DC

TEEN TITANS GO!™

FOOD FRIGHT AND PAR FOR THE COURSE

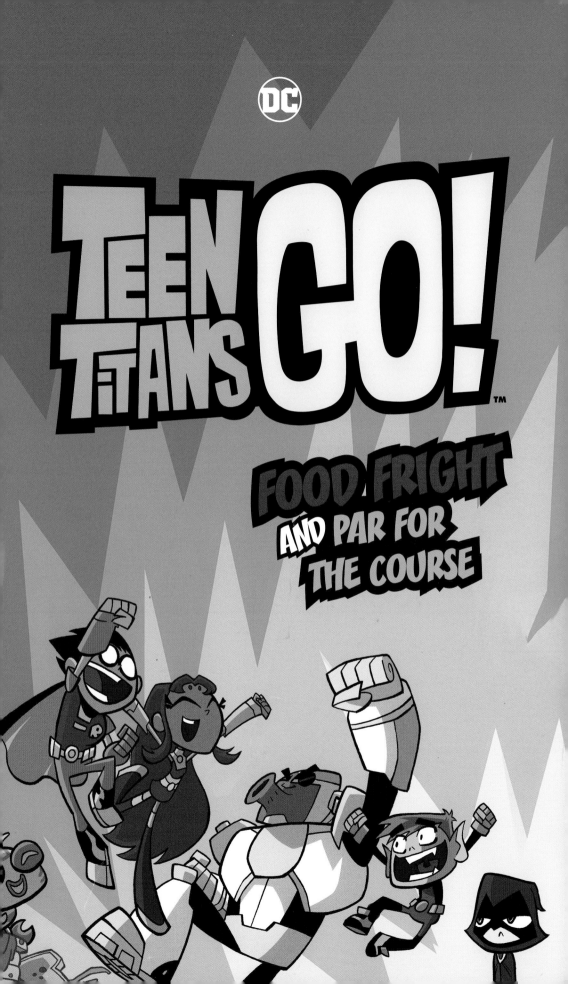

Teen Titans Go! is published by
Stone Arch Books,
A Capstone Imprint
1710 Roe Crest Drive
North Mankato, MN 56003
www.mycapstonepub.com

Library of Congress Cataloging-in-Publication Data is available at the Library of Congress website:
ISBN: 978-1-4965-7993-5 (library binding)
ISBN: 978-1-4965-7999-7 (eBook PDF)

Summary: Someone's been eating Cyborg's sandwiches! But who? One of the other Teen Titans? Or something more . . .
SINISTER? Cyborg and his stomach want answers! NOW! Then tempers flare as Beast Boy, Robin, and Cyborg enjoy a
"friendly" game of mini-golf. Meanwhile Raven and Starfire hit the arcade.

Alex Antone Editor – Original Series Paul Santos Editor

STONE ARCH BOOKS
Chris Harbo Editor
Brann Garvey Designer
Hilary Wacholz Art Director
Kathy McColley Production Specialist

Printed and bound in the USA
1965

TEEN TITANS GO!™

SHOLLY FISCH MERRILL HAGAN
WRITERS

BEN BATES JORGE CORONA
ARTISTS

JEREMY LAWSON
COLORIST

WES ABBOTT
LETTERER

DAN HIPP
COVER ARTIST

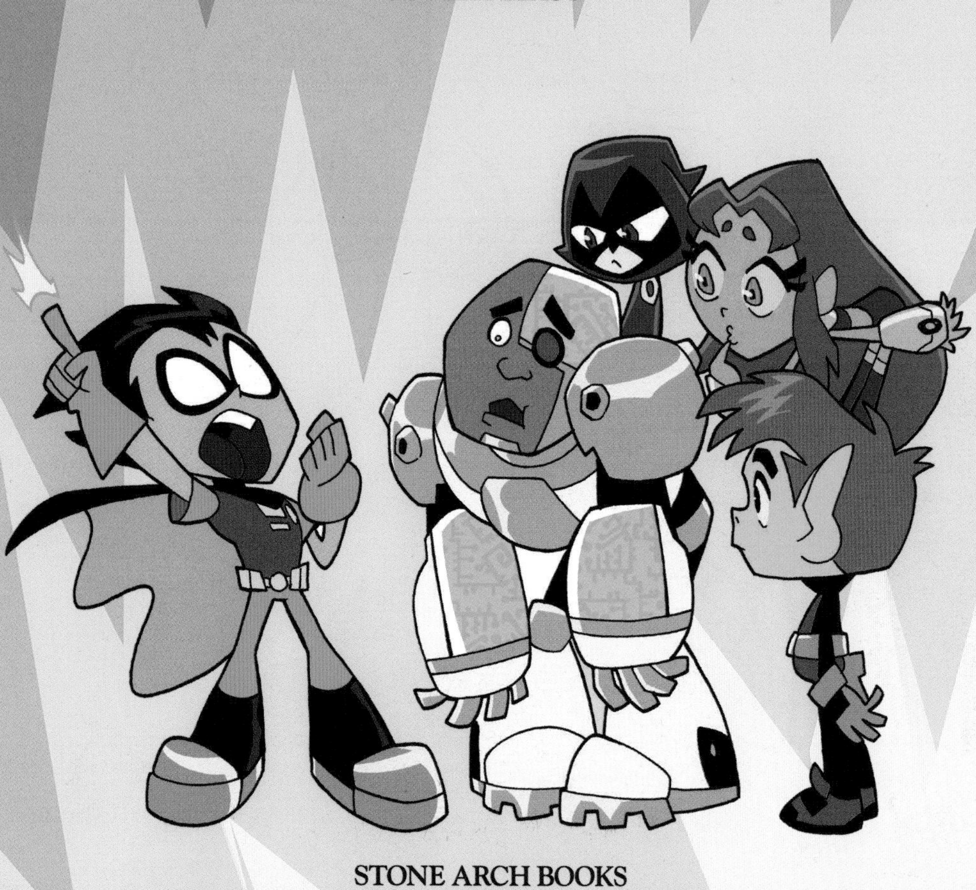

STONE ARCH BOOKS
a capstone imprint

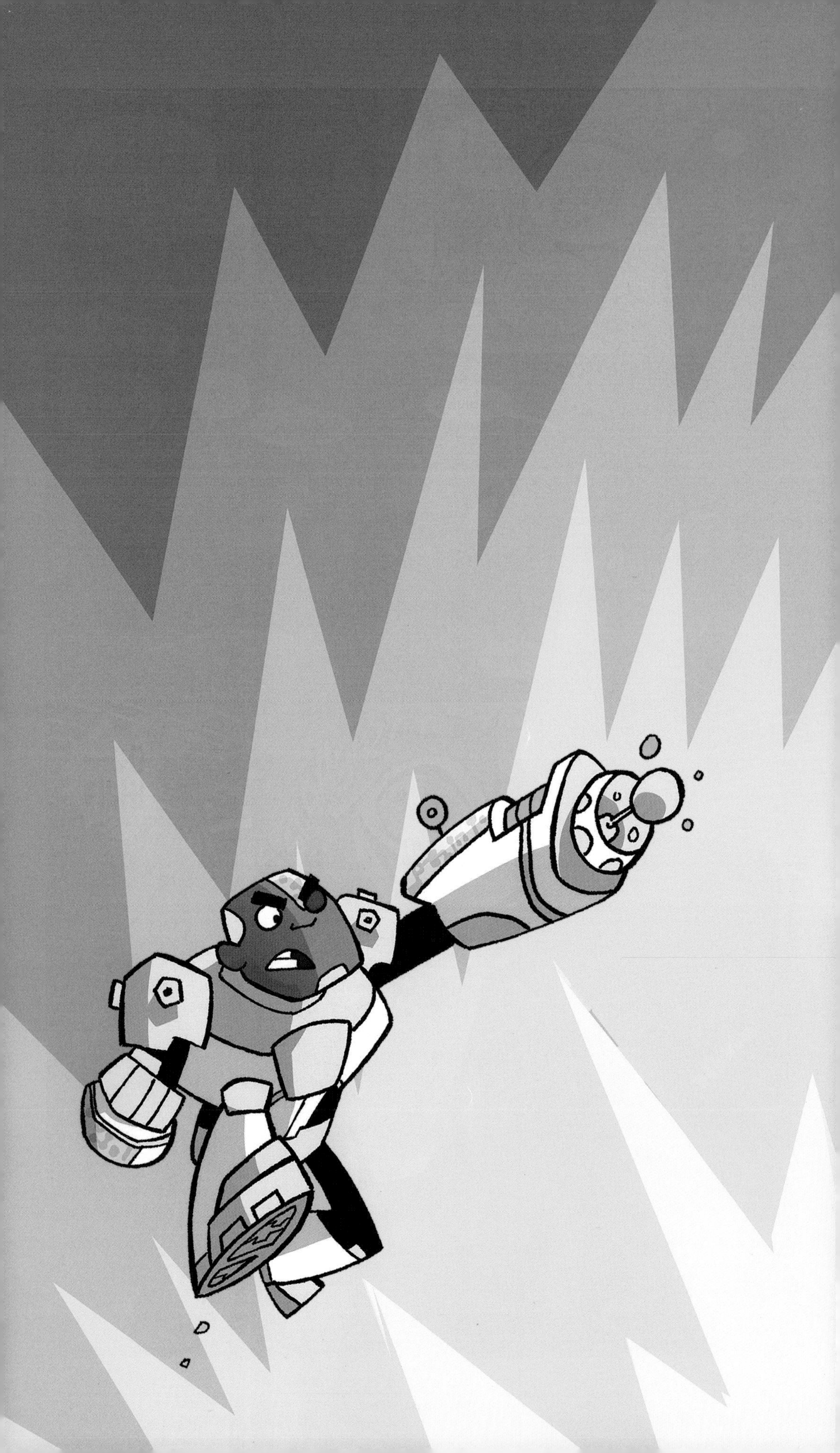

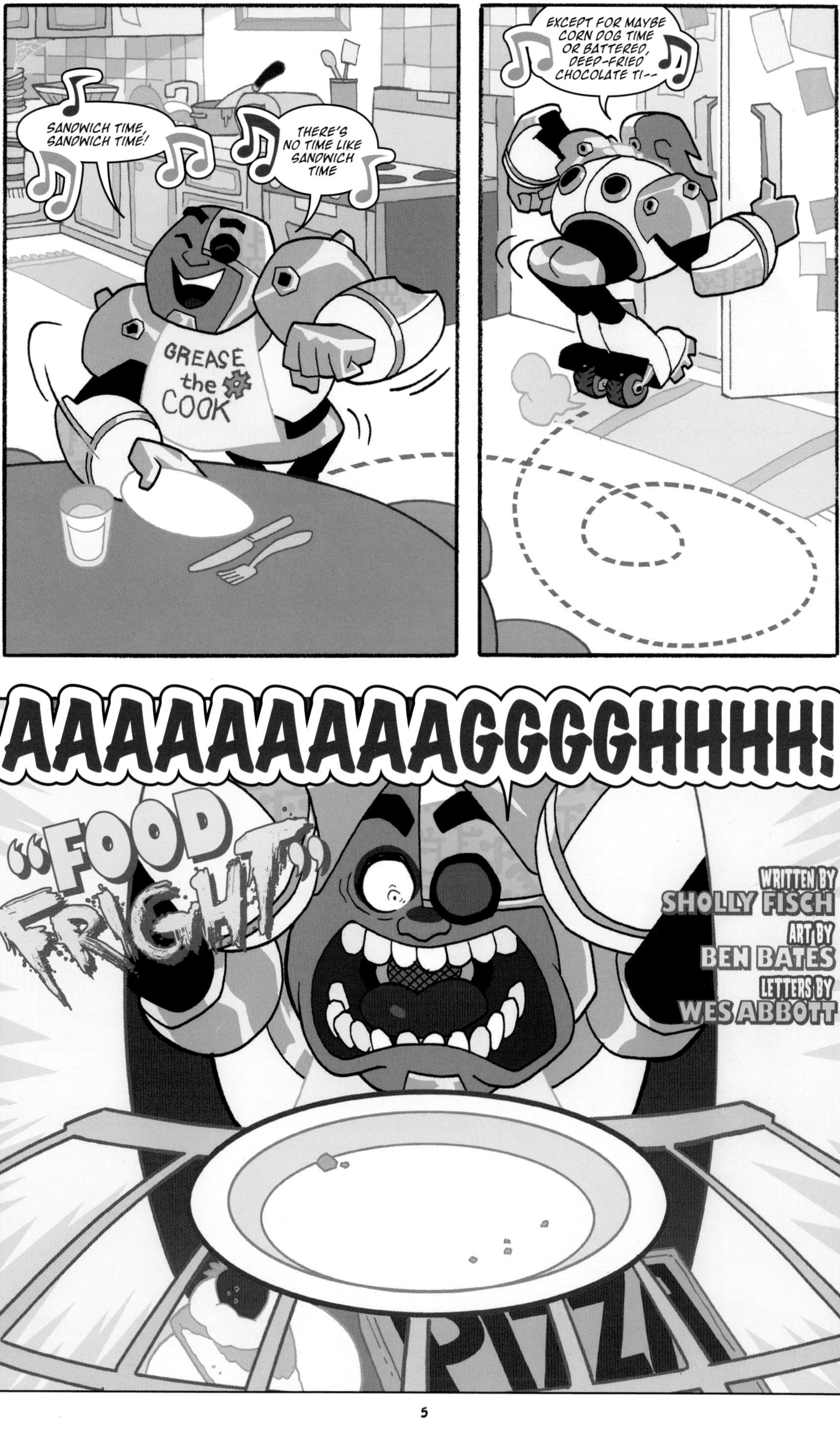
SANDWICH TIME, SANDWICH TIME!
THERE'S NO TIME LIKE SANDWICH TIME
GREASE the COOK
EXCEPT FOR MAYBE CORN DOG TIME OR BATTERED, DEEP-FRIED CHOCOLATE TI--
AAAAAAAAAAGGGGHHHH!
"FOOD FRIGHT"
WRITTEN BY SHOLLY FISCH
ART BY BEN BATES
LETTERS BY WES ABBOTT

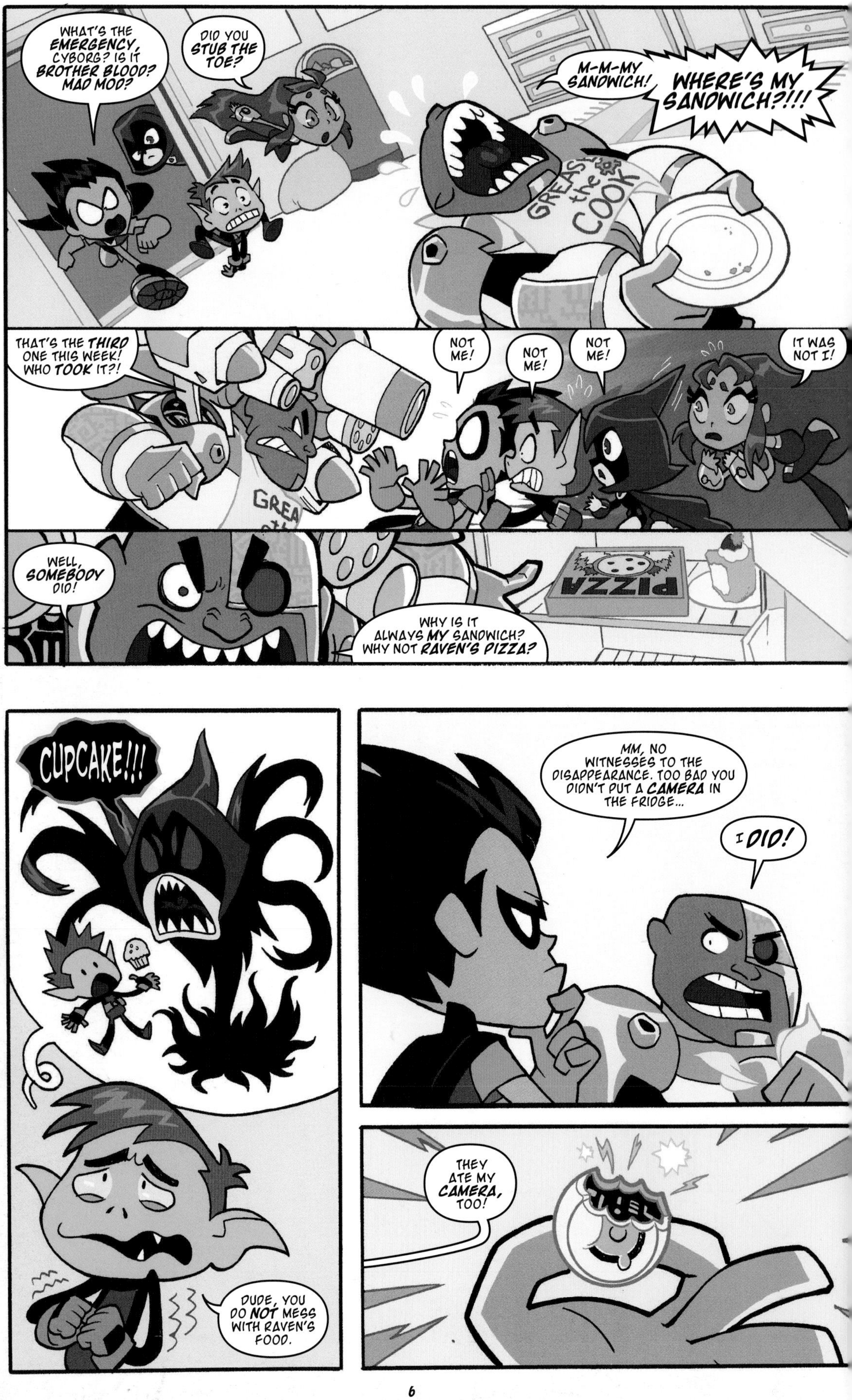
WHAT'S THE EMERGENCY, CYBORG? IS IT BROTHER BLOOD? MAD MOD?
DID YOU STUB THE TOE?
M-M-MY SANDWICH!
WHERE'S MY SANDWICH?!!!
GREASY the COOK
THAT'S THE THIRD ONE THIS WEEK! WHO TOOK IT?!
NOT ME!
NOT ME!
NOT ME!
IT WAS NOT I!
WELL, SOMEBODY DID!
PIZZA
WHY IS IT ALWAYS MY SANDWICH? WHY NOT RAVEN'S PIZZA?
CUPCAKE!!!
DUDE, YOU DO NOT MESS WITH RAVEN'S FOOD.
MM, NO WITNESSES TO THE DISAPPEARANCE. TOO BAD YOU DIDN'T PUT A CAMERA IN THE FRIDGE...
I DID!
THEY ATE MY CAMERA, TOO!

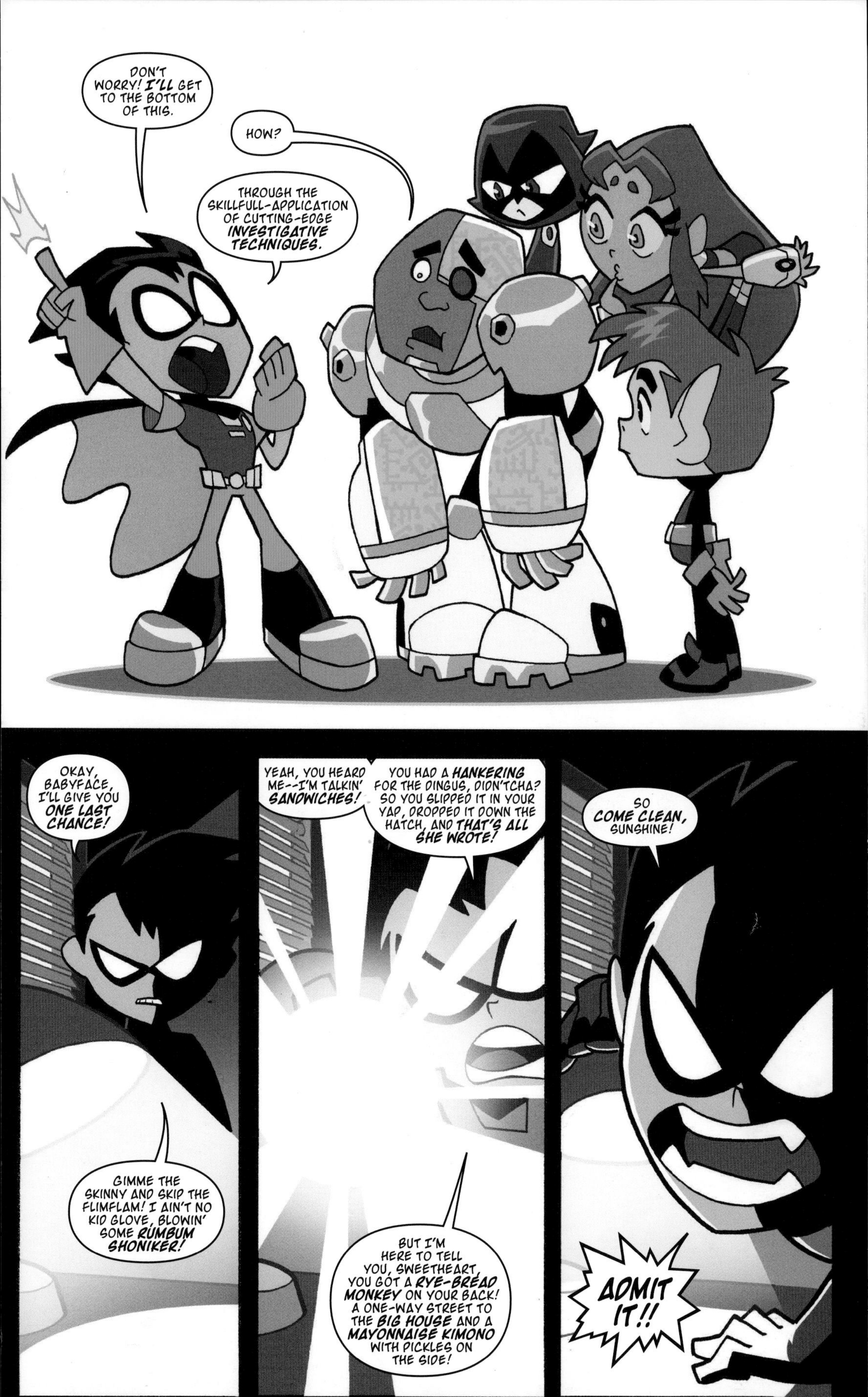

DON'T WORRY! I'LL GET TO THE BOTTOM OF THIS.
HOW?
THROUGH THE SKILLFULL-APPLICATION OF CUTTING-EDGE INVESTIGATIVE TECHNIQUES.
OKAY, BABYFACE, I'LL GIVE YOU ONE LAST CHANCE!
GIMME THE SKINNY AND SKIP THE FLIMFLAM! I AIN'T NO KID GLOVE, BLOWIN' SOME RUMBUM SHONIKER!
YEAH, YOU HEARD ME--I'M TALKIN' SANDWICHES!
YOU HAD A HANKERING FOR THE DINGUS, DIDN'TCHA? SO YOU SLIPPED IT IN YOUR YAP, DROPPED IT DOWN THE HATCH, AND THAT'S ALL SHE WROTE!
BUT I'M HERE TO TELL YOU, SWEETHEART, YOU GOT A RYE-BREAD MONKEY ON YOUR BACK! A ONE-WAY STREET TO THE BIG HOUSE AND A MAYONNAISE KIMONO WITH PICKLES ON THE SIDE!
SO COME CLEAN, SUNSHINE!
ADMIT IT!!

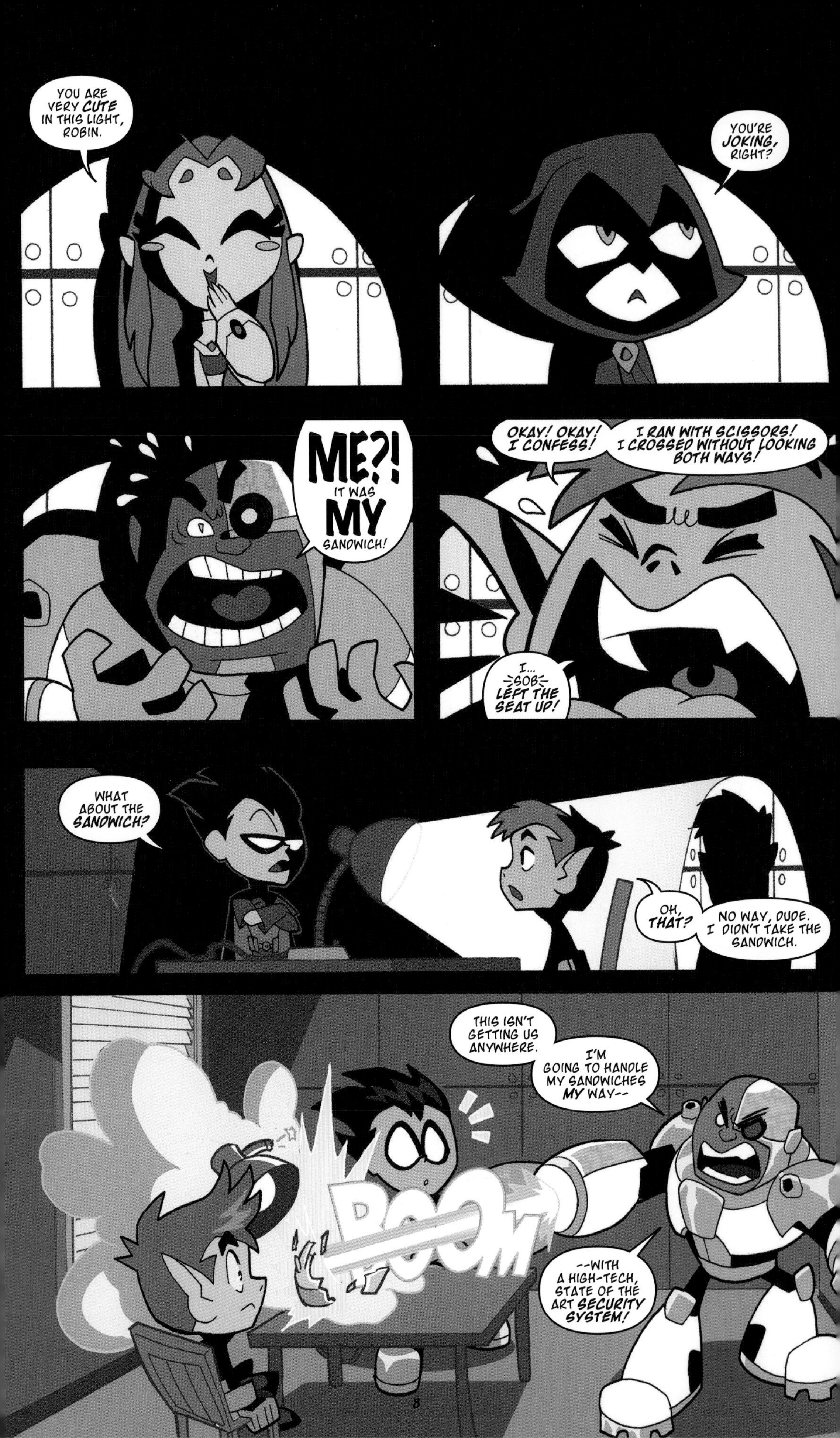
YOU ARE VERY CUTE IN THIS LIGHT, ROBIN.
YOU'RE JOKING, RIGHT?
ME?! IT WAS MY SANDWICH!
OKAY! OKAY! I CONFESS!
I RAN WITH SCISSORS! I CROSSED WITHOUT LOOKING BOTH WAYS!
I... -SOB- LEFT THE SEAT UP!
WHAT ABOUT THE SANDWICH?
OH, THAT?
NO WAY, DUDE. I DIDN'T TAKE THE SANDWICH.
THIS ISN'T GETTING US ANYWHERE.
I'M GOING TO HANDLE MY SANDWICHES MY WAY--
BOOM
--WITH A HIGH-TECH, STATE OF THE ART SECURITY SYSTEM!

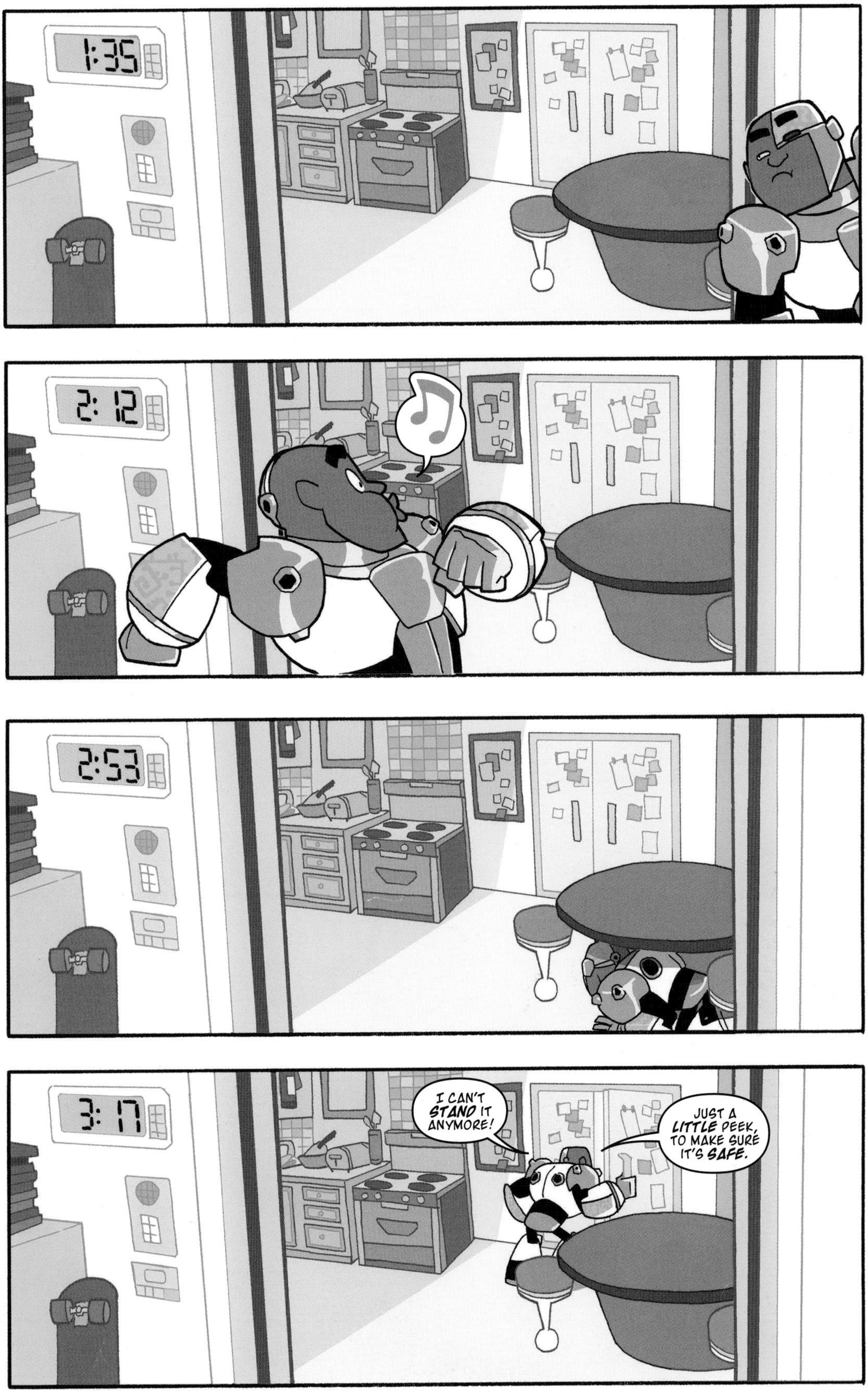
1:35
2:12
2:53
3:17
I CAN'T STAND IT ANYMORE!
JUST A LITTLE PEEK, TO MAKE SURE IT'S SAFE.

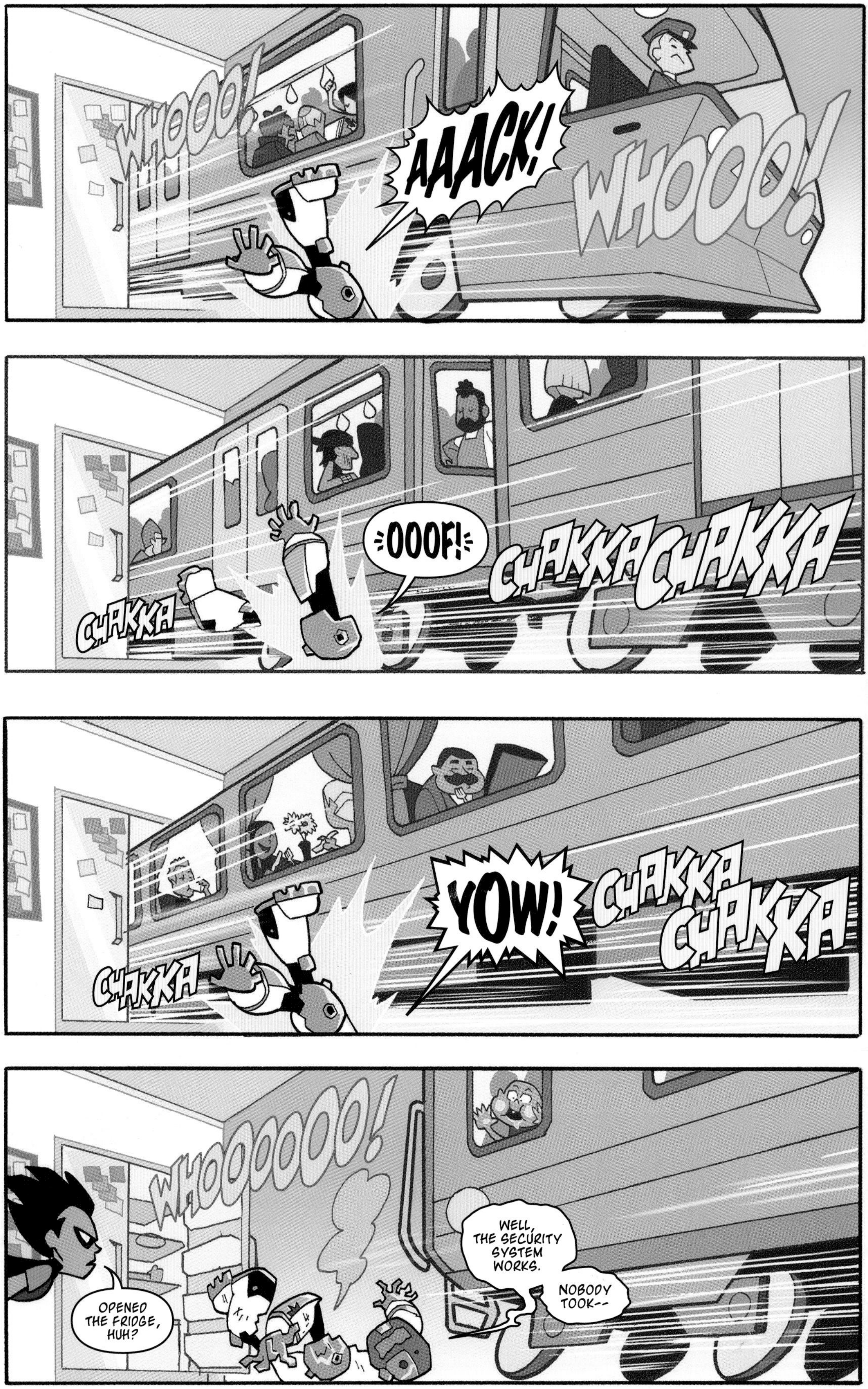
WHOOO!
AAACK!
WHOOO!
CHAKKA
OOOF!
CHAKKA CHAKKA
CHAKKA
YOW!
CHAKKA CHAKKA
WHOOOOOO!
OPENED THE FRIDGE, HUH?
WELL, THE SECURITY SYSTEM WORKS.
NOBODY TOOK--

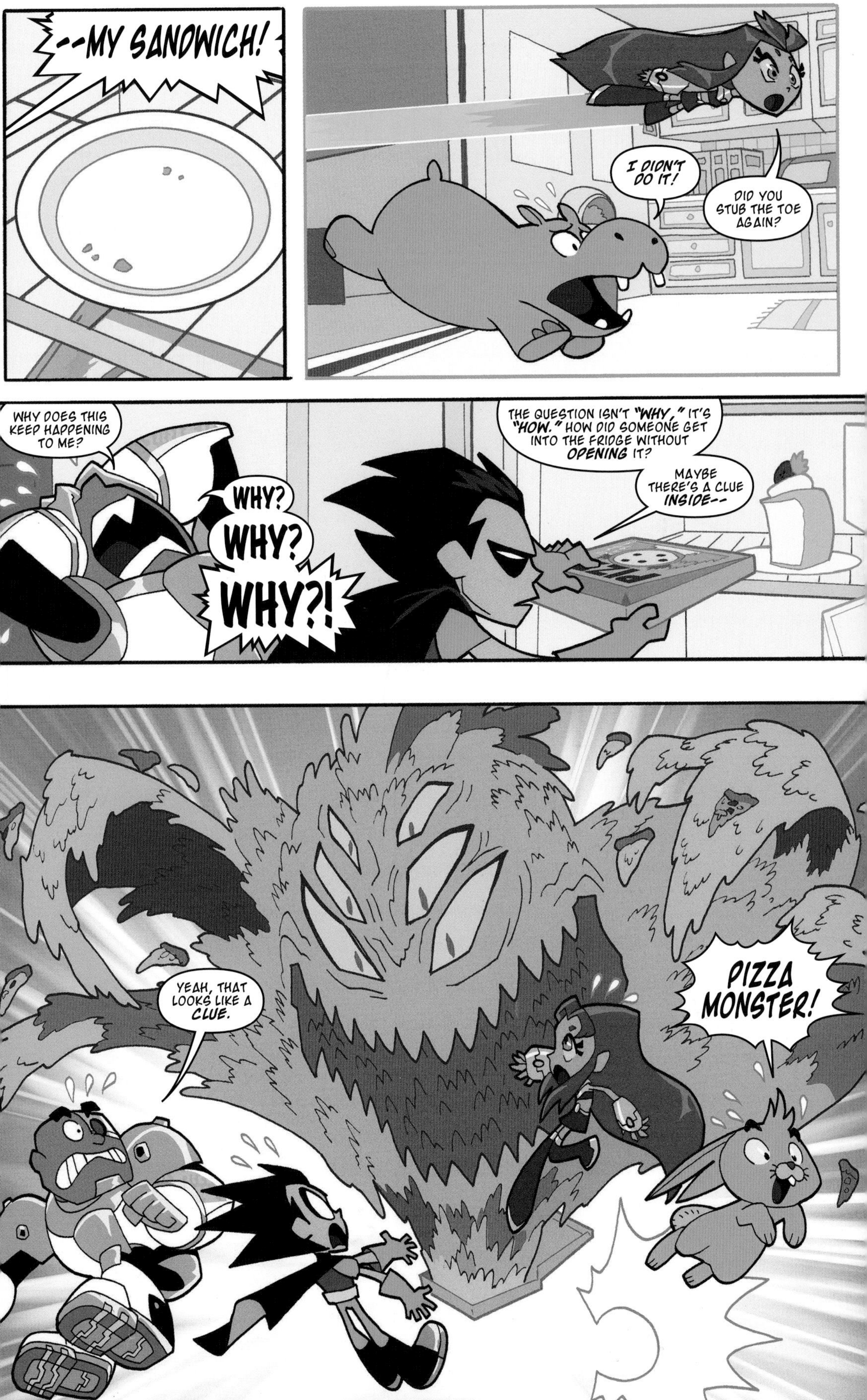
--MY SANDWICH!
I DIDN'T DO IT!
DID YOU STUB THE TOE AGAIN?
WHY DOES THIS KEEP HAPPENING TO ME?
WHY?
WHY?
WHY?!
THE QUESTION ISN'T "WHY," IT'S "HOW." HOW DID SOMEONE GET INTO THE FRIDGE WITHOUT OPENING IT?
MAYBE THERE'S A CLUE INSIDE--
YEAH, THAT LOOKS LIKE A CLUE.
PIZZA MONSTER!

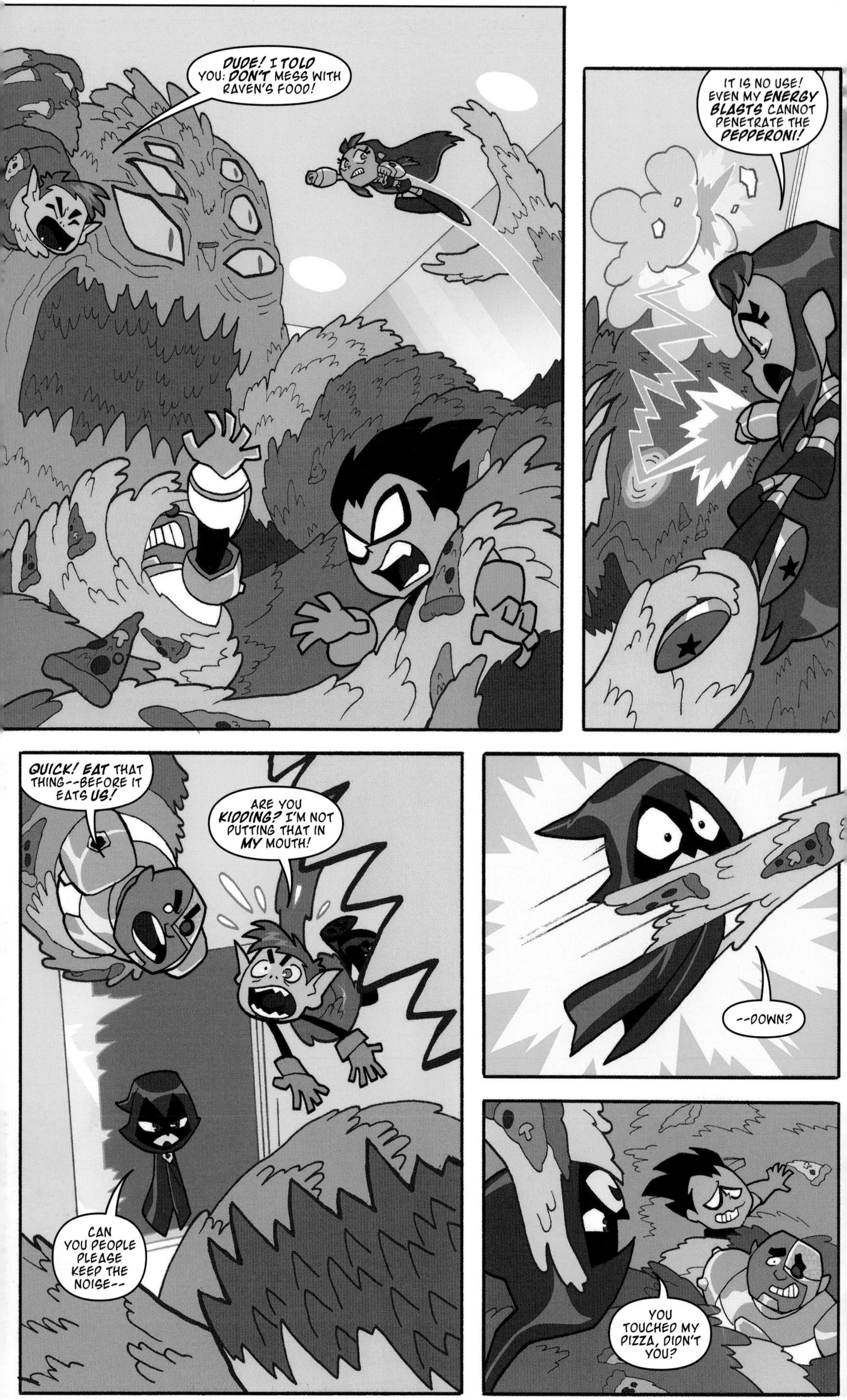
DUDE! I TOLD YOU: DON'T MESS WITH RAVEN'S FOOD!
IT IS NO USE! EVEN MY ENERGY BLASTS CANNOT PENETRATE THE PEPPERONI!
QUICK! EAT THAT THING--BEFORE IT EATS US!
ARE YOU KIDDING? I'M NOT PUTTING THAT IN MY MOUTH!
CAN YOU PEOPLE PLEASE KEEP THE NOISE--
--DOWN?
YOU TOUCHED MY PIZZA, DIDN'T YOU?

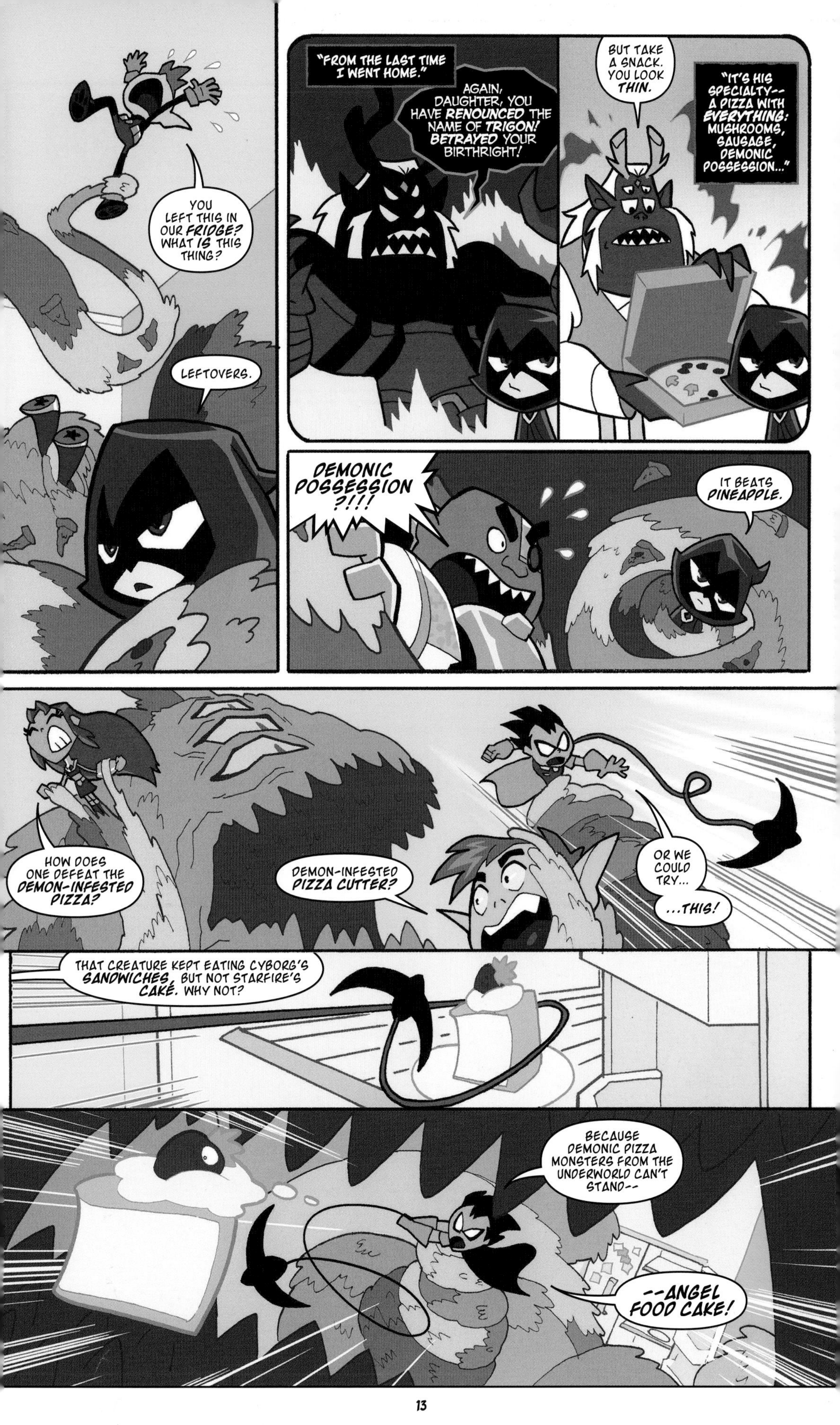
YOU LEFT THIS IN OUR FRIDGE? WHAT IS THIS THING?
LEFTOVERS.
"FROM THE LAST TIME I WENT HOME."
AGAIN, DAUGHTER, YOU HAVE RENOUNCED THE NAME OF TRIGON! BETRAYED YOUR BIRTHRIGHT!
BUT TAKE A SNACK. YOU LOOK THIN.
"IT'S HIS SPECIALTY-- A PIZZA WITH EVERYTHING: MUSHROOMS, SAUSAGE, DEMONIC POSSESSION..."
DEMONIC POSSESSION ?!!!
IT BEATS PINEAPPLE.
HOW DOES ONE DEFEAT THE DEMON-INFESTED PIZZA?
DEMON-INFESTED PIZZA CUTTER?
OR WE COULD TRY...
...THIS!
THAT CREATURE KEPT EATING CYBORG'S SANDWICHES, BUT NOT STARFIRE'S CAKE. WHY NOT?
BECAUSE DEMONIC PIZZA MONSTERS FROM THE UNDERWORLD CAN'T STAND--
--ANGEL FOOD CAKE!

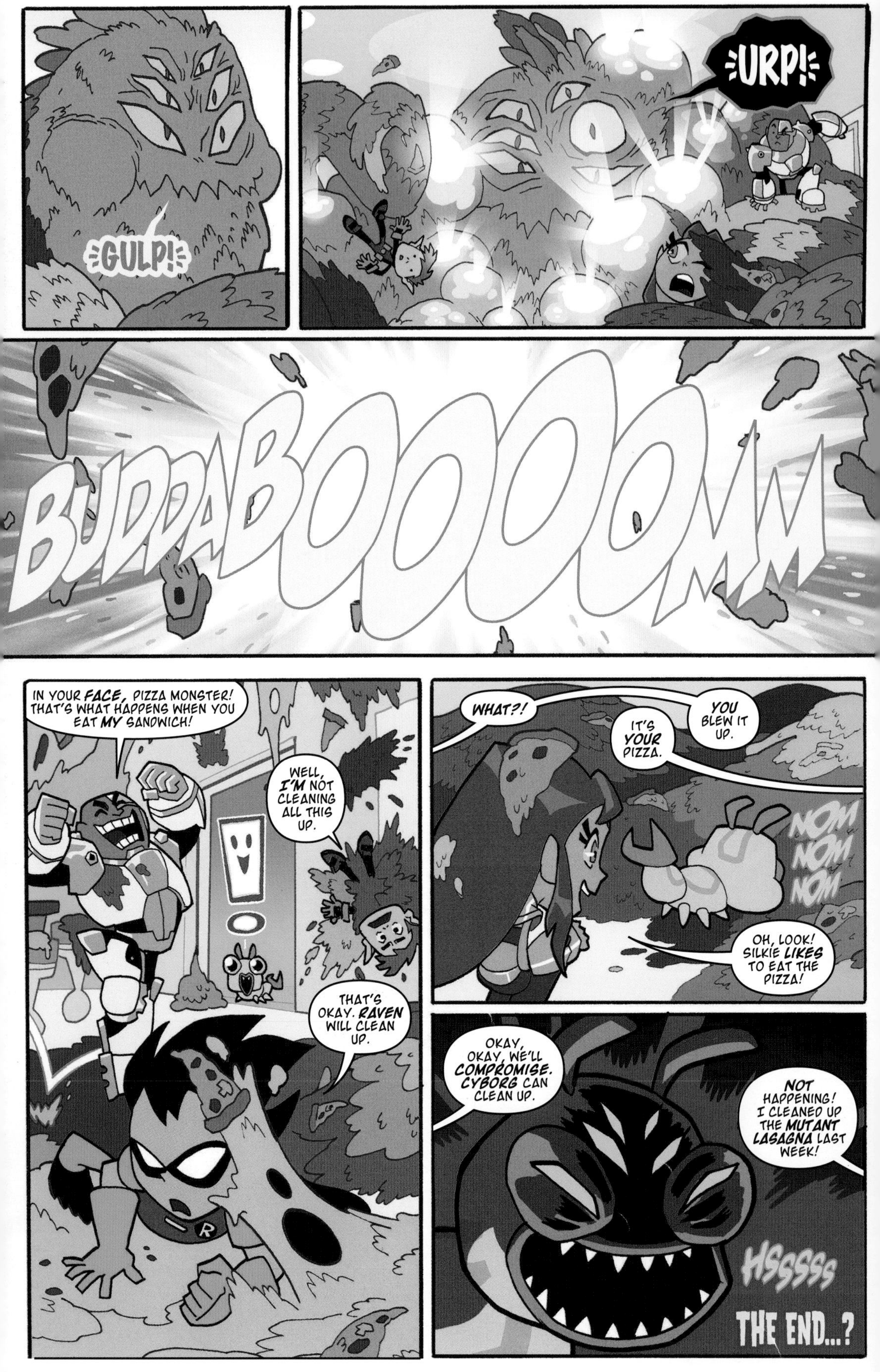
GULP!
URP!
BUDDABOOOOOMM
IN YOUR FACE, PIZZA MONSTER! THAT'S WHAT HAPPENS WHEN YOU EAT MY SANDWICH!
WELL, I'M NOT CLEANING ALL THIS UP.
THAT'S OKAY. RAVEN WILL CLEAN UP.
WHAT?!
IT'S YOUR PIZZA.
YOU BLEW IT UP.
NOM NOM NOM
OH, LOOK! SILKIE LIKES TO EAT THE PIZZA!
OKAY, OKAY, WE'LL COMPROMISE. CYBORG CAN CLEAN UP.
NOT HAPPENING! I CLEANED UP THE MUTANT LASAGNA LAST WEEK!
HSSSSS
THE END...?

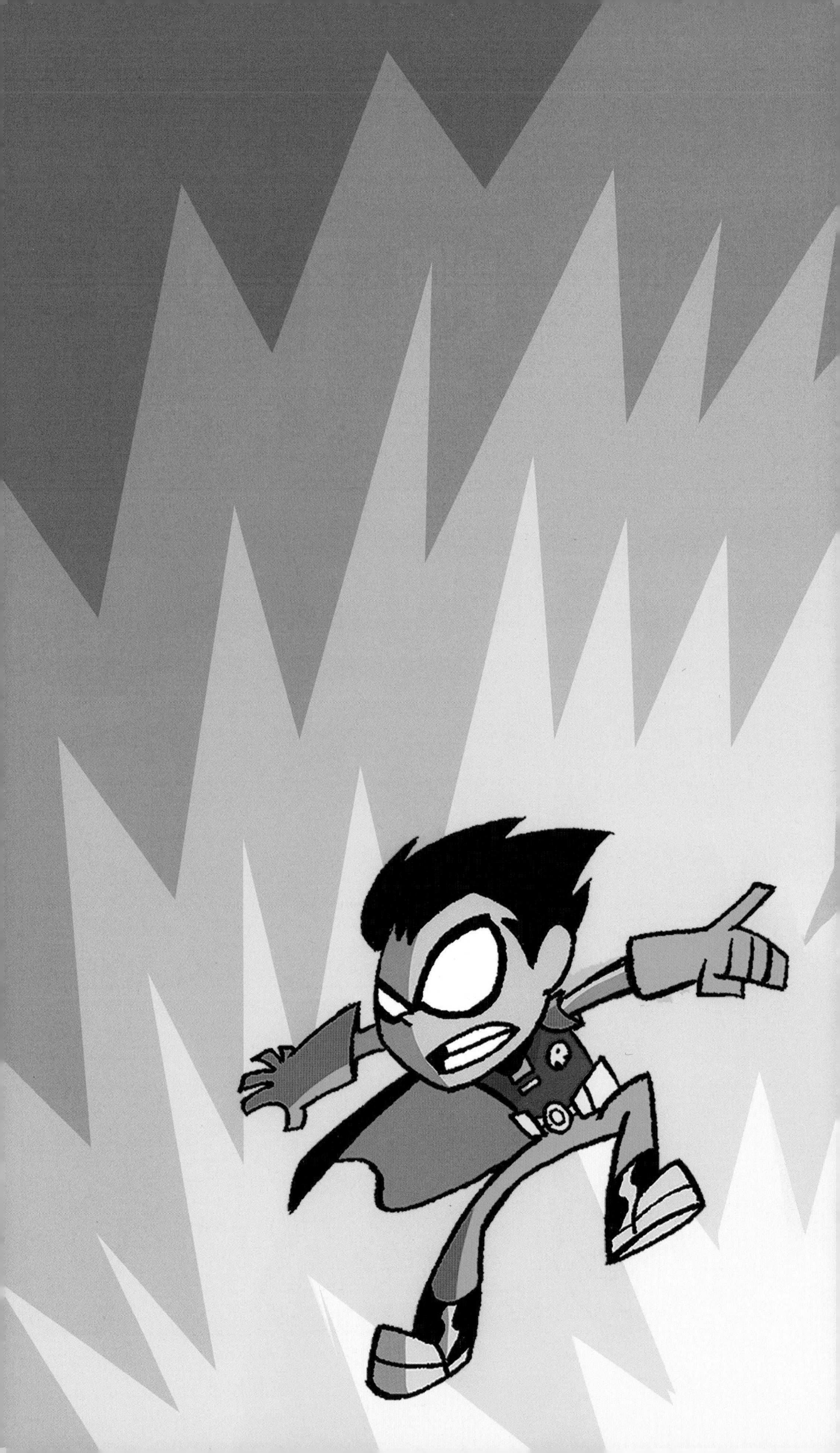

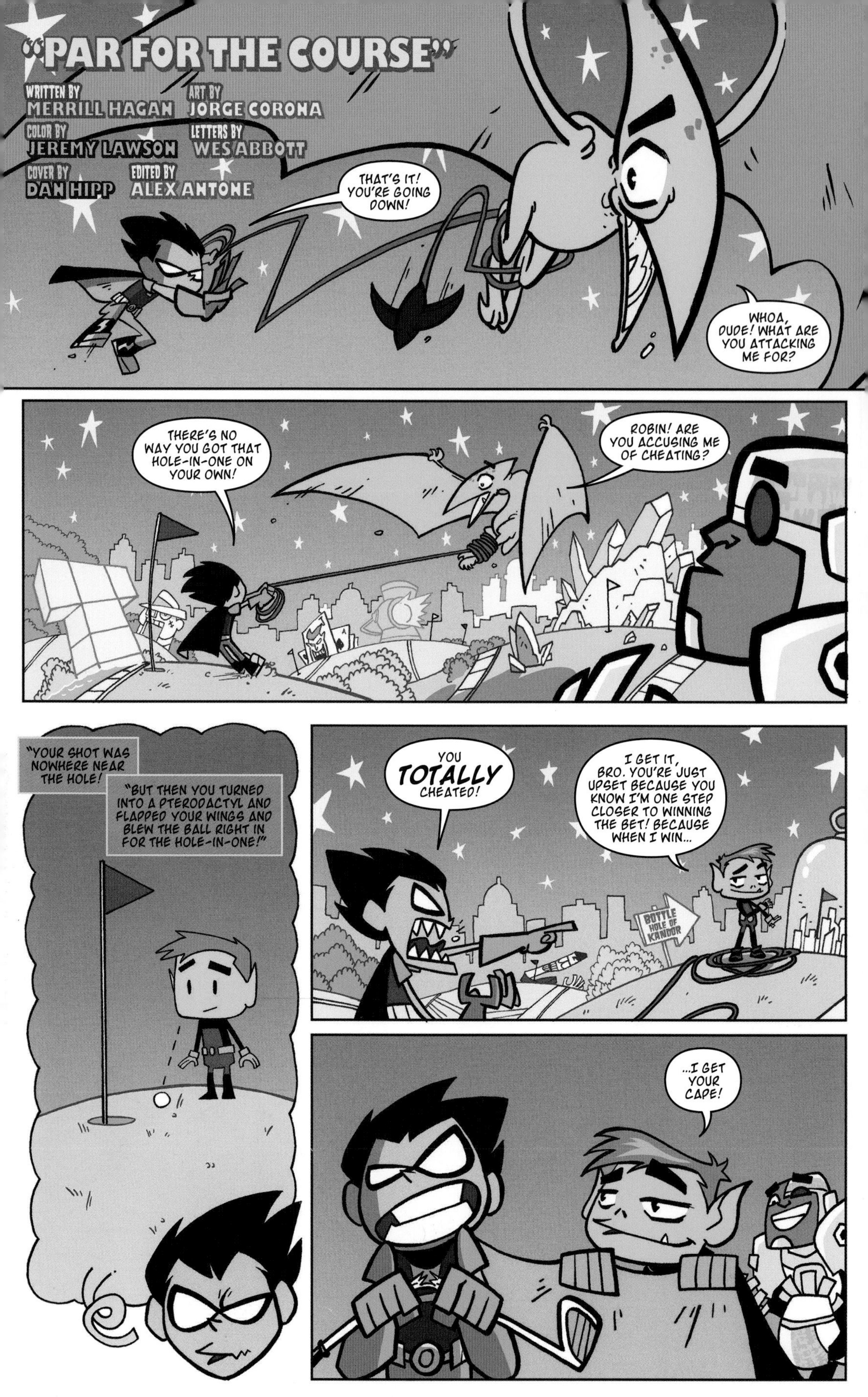
"PAR FOR THE COURSE"
WRITTEN BY MERRILL HAGAN
ART BY JORGE CORONA
COLOR BY JEREMY LAWSON
LETTERS BY WES ABBOTT
COVER BY DAN HIPP
EDITED BY ALEX ANTONE
THAT'S IT! YOU'RE GOING DOWN!
WHOA, DUDE! WHAT ARE YOU ATTACKING ME FOR?
THERE'S NO WAY YOU GOT THAT HOLE-IN-ONE ON YOUR OWN!
ROBIN! ARE YOU ACCUSING ME OF CHEATING?
"YOUR SHOT WAS NOWHERE NEAR THE HOLE!
"BUT THEN YOU TURNED INTO A PTERODACTYL AND FLAPPED YOUR WINGS AND BLEW THE BALL RIGHT IN FOR THE HOLE-IN-ONE!"
YOU TOTALLY CHEATED!
I GET IT, BRO. YOU'RE JUST UPSET BECAUSE YOU KNOW I'M ONE STEP CLOSER TO WINNING THE BET! BECAUSE WHEN I WIN...
BOTTLE HOLE OF KANDOR
...I GET YOUR CAPE!

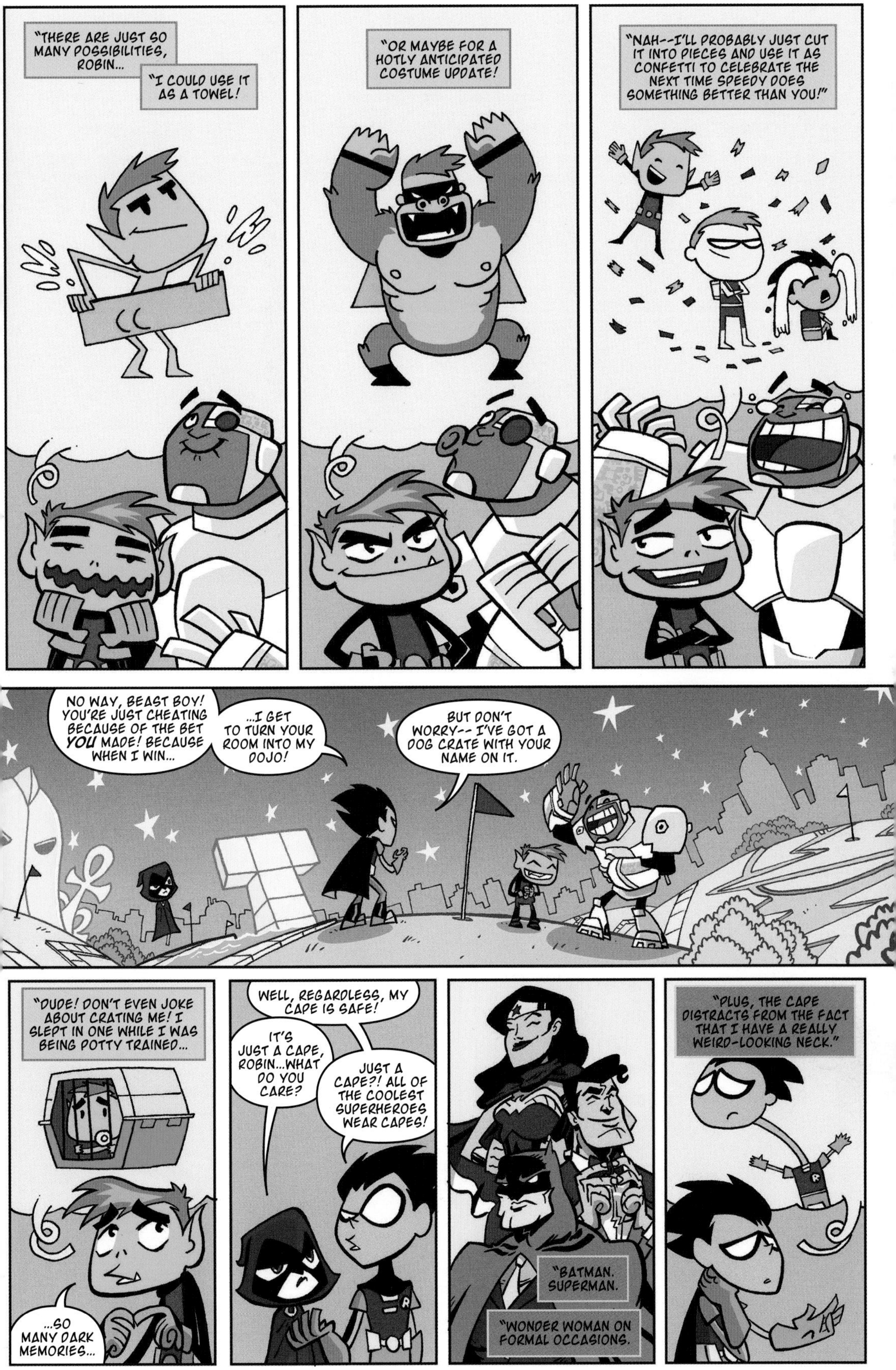
"THERE ARE JUST SO MANY POSSIBILITIES, ROBIN...
"I COULD USE IT AS A TOWEL!
"OR MAYBE FOR A HOTLY ANTICIPATED COSTUME UPDATE!
"NAH--I'LL PROBABLY JUST CUT IT INTO PIECES AND USE IT AS CONFETTI TO CELEBRATE THE NEXT TIME SPEEDY DOES SOMETHING BETTER THAN YOU!"
NO WAY, BEAST BOY! YOU'RE JUST CHEATING BECAUSE OF THE BET YOU MADE! BECAUSE WHEN I WIN...
...I GET TO TURN YOUR ROOM INTO MY DOJO!
BUT DON'T WORRY-- I'VE GOT A DOG CRATE WITH YOUR NAME ON IT.
"DUDE! DON'T EVEN JOKE ABOUT CRATING ME! I SLEPT IN ONE WHILE I WAS BEING POTTY TRAINED...
...SO MANY DARK MEMORIES...
WELL, REGARDLESS, MY CAPE IS SAFE!
IT'S JUST A CAPE, ROBIN...WHAT DO YOU CARE?
JUST A CAPE?! ALL OF THE COOLEST SUPERHEROES WEAR CAPES!
"BATMAN. SUPERMAN.
"WONDER WOMAN ON FORMAL OCCASIONS.
"PLUS, THE CAPE DISTRACTS FROM THE FACT THAT I HAVE A REALLY WEIRD-LOOKING NECK."

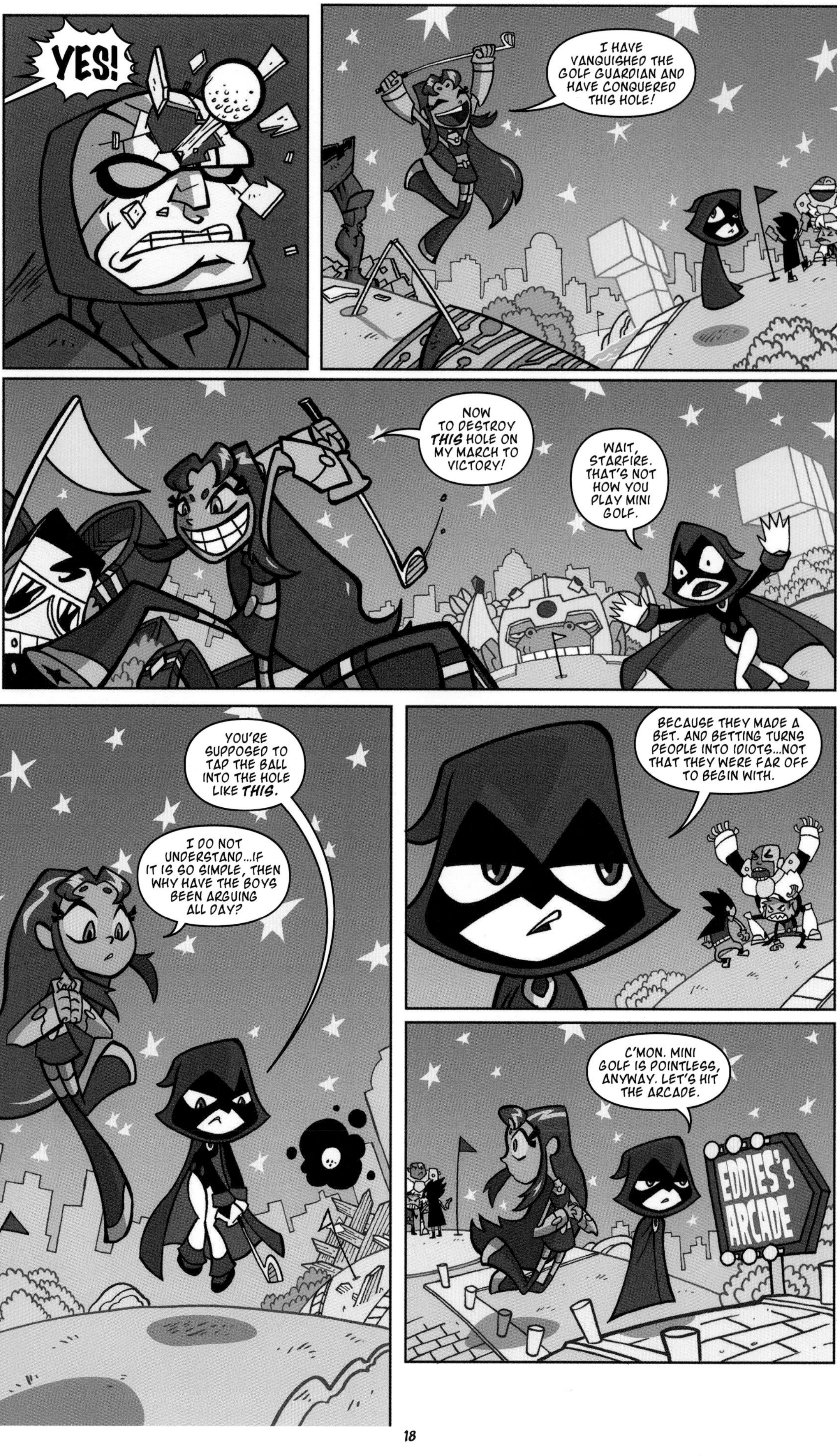
YES!
I HAVE VANQUISHED THE GOLF GUARDIAN AND HAVE CONQUERED THIS HOLE!
NOW TO DESTROY THIS HOLE ON MY MARCH TO VICTORY!
WAIT, STARFIRE. THAT'S NOT HOW YOU PLAY MINI GOLF.
YOU'RE SUPPOSED TO TAP THE BALL INTO THE HOLE LIKE THIS.
I DO NOT UNDERSTAND...IF IT IS SO SIMPLE, THEN WHY HAVE THE BOYS BEEN ARGUING ALL DAY?
BECAUSE THEY MADE A BET. AND BETTING TURNS PEOPLE INTO IDIOTS...NOT THAT THEY WERE FAR OFF TO BEGIN WITH.
C'MON. MINI GOLF IS POINTLESS, ANYWAY. LET'S HIT THE ARCADE.
EDDIES'S ARCADE

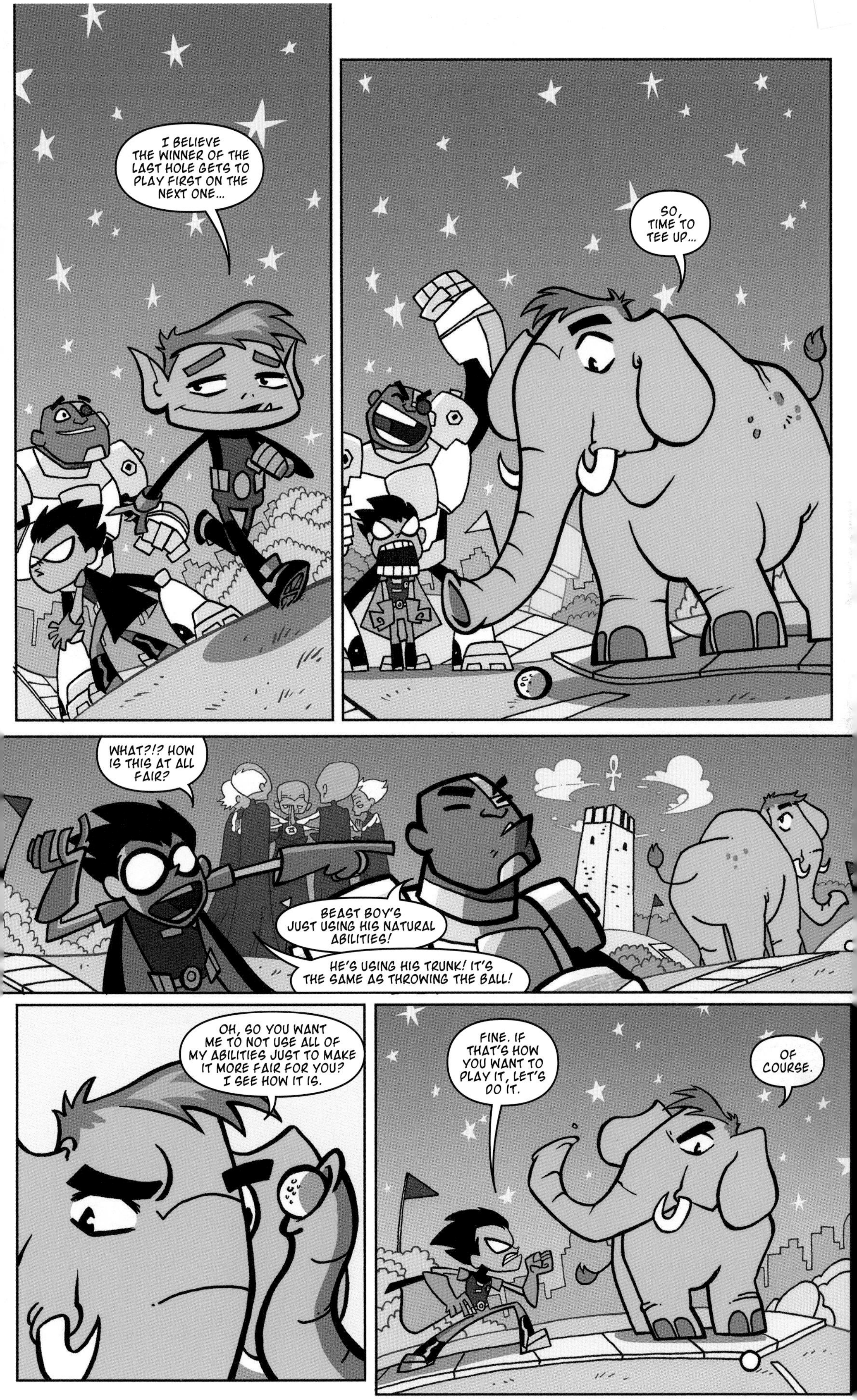
I BELIEVE THE WINNER OF THE LAST HOLE GETS TO PLAY FIRST ON THE NEXT ONE...
SO, TIME TO TEE UP...
WHAT?!? HOW IS THIS AT ALL FAIR?
BEAST BOY'S JUST USING HIS NATURAL ABILITIES!
HE'S USING HIS TRUNK! IT'S THE SAME AS THROWING THE BALL!
OH, SO YOU WANT ME TO NOT USE ALL OF MY ABILITIES JUST TO MAKE IT MORE FAIR FOR YOU? I SEE HOW IT IS.
FINE. IF THAT'S HOW YOU WANT TO PLAY IT, LET'S DO IT.
OF COURSE.

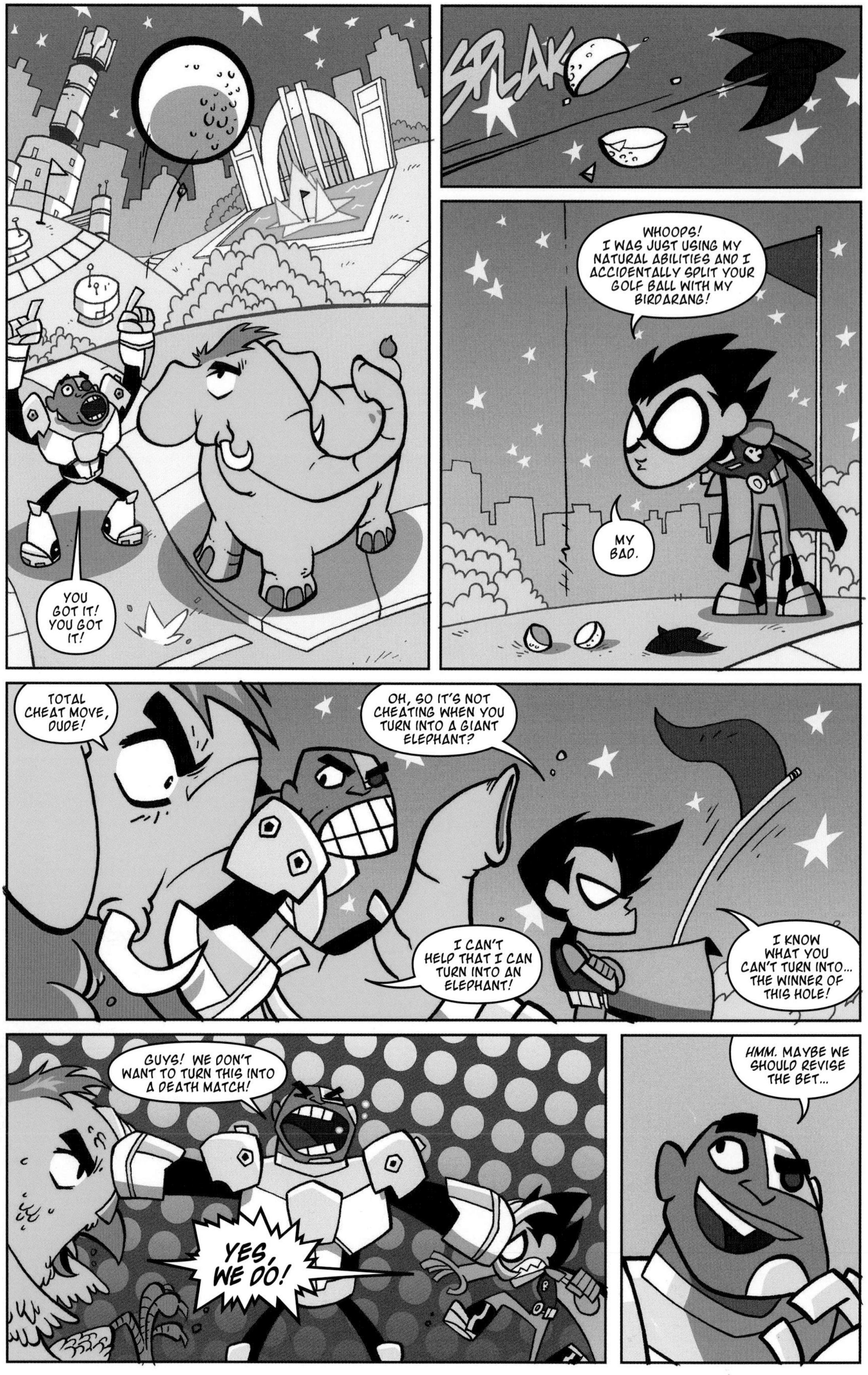
SPLAK
WHOOPS! I WAS JUST USING MY NATURAL ABILITIES AND I ACCIDENTALLY SPLIT YOUR GOLF BALL WITH MY BIRDARANG!
YOU GOT IT! YOU GOT IT!
MY BAD.
TOTAL CHEAT MOVE, DUDE!
OH, SO IT'S NOT CHEATING WHEN YOU TURN INTO A GIANT ELEPHANT?
I CAN'T HELP THAT I CAN TURN INTO AN ELEPHANT!
I KNOW WHAT YOU CAN'T TURN INTO... THE WINNER OF THIS HOLE!
GUYS! WE DON'T WANT TO TURN THIS INTO A DEATH MATCH!
YES, WE DO!
HMM. MAYBE WE SHOULD REVISE THE BET...

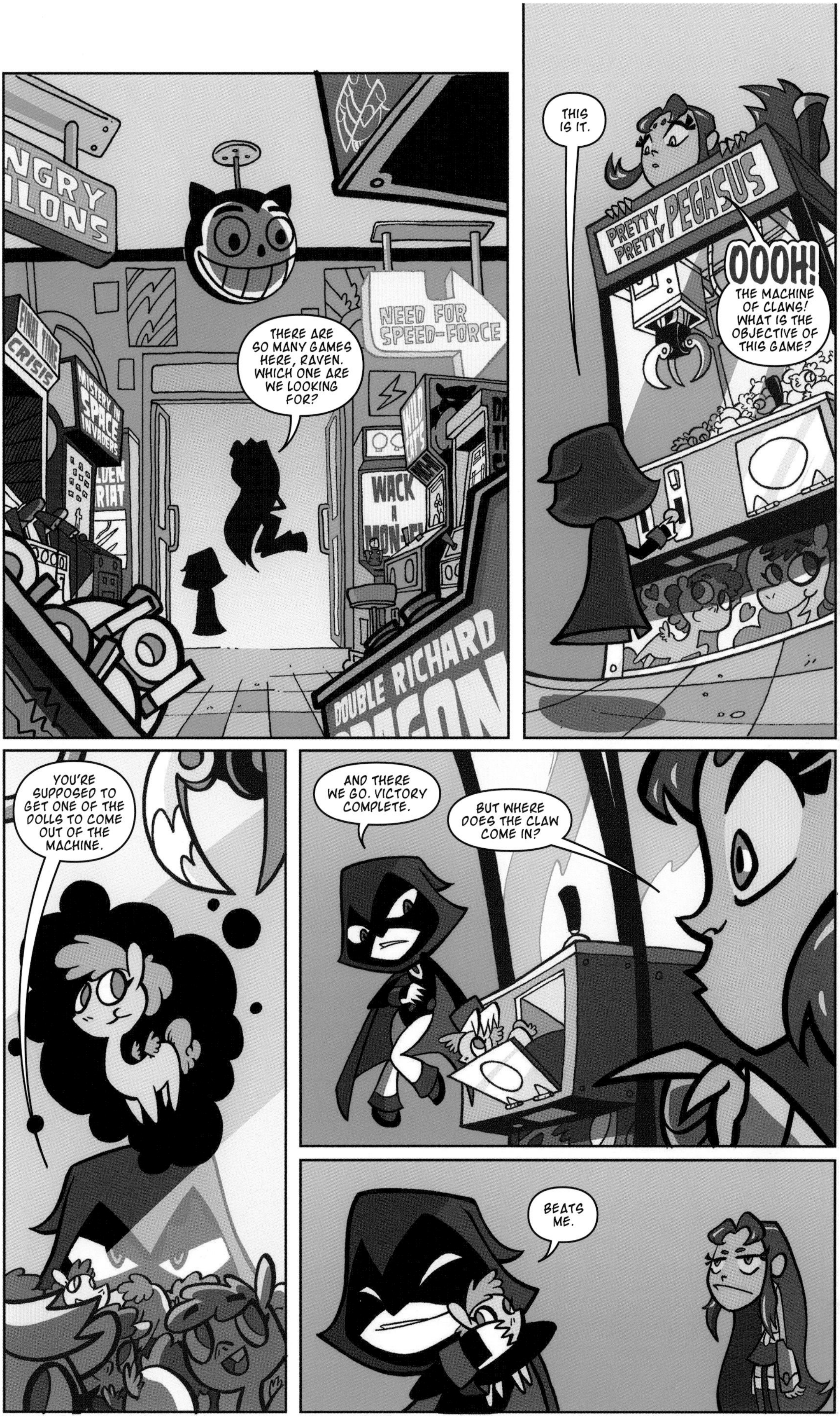
NEED FOR SPEED-FORCE
FINAL TIME CRISIS
MYSTERY IN SPACE INVADERS
DOUBLE RICHARD
THERE ARE SO MANY GAMES HERE, RAVEN. WHICH ONE ARE WE LOOKING FOR?
THIS IS IT.
PRETTY PRETTY PEGASUS
OOOH! THE MACHINE OF CLAWS! WHAT IS THE OBJECTIVE OF THIS GAME?
YOU'RE SUPPOSED TO GET ONE OF THE DOLLS TO COME OUT OF THE MACHINE.
AND THERE WE GO. VICTORY COMPLETE.
BUT WHERE DOES THE CLAW COME IN?
BEATS ME.

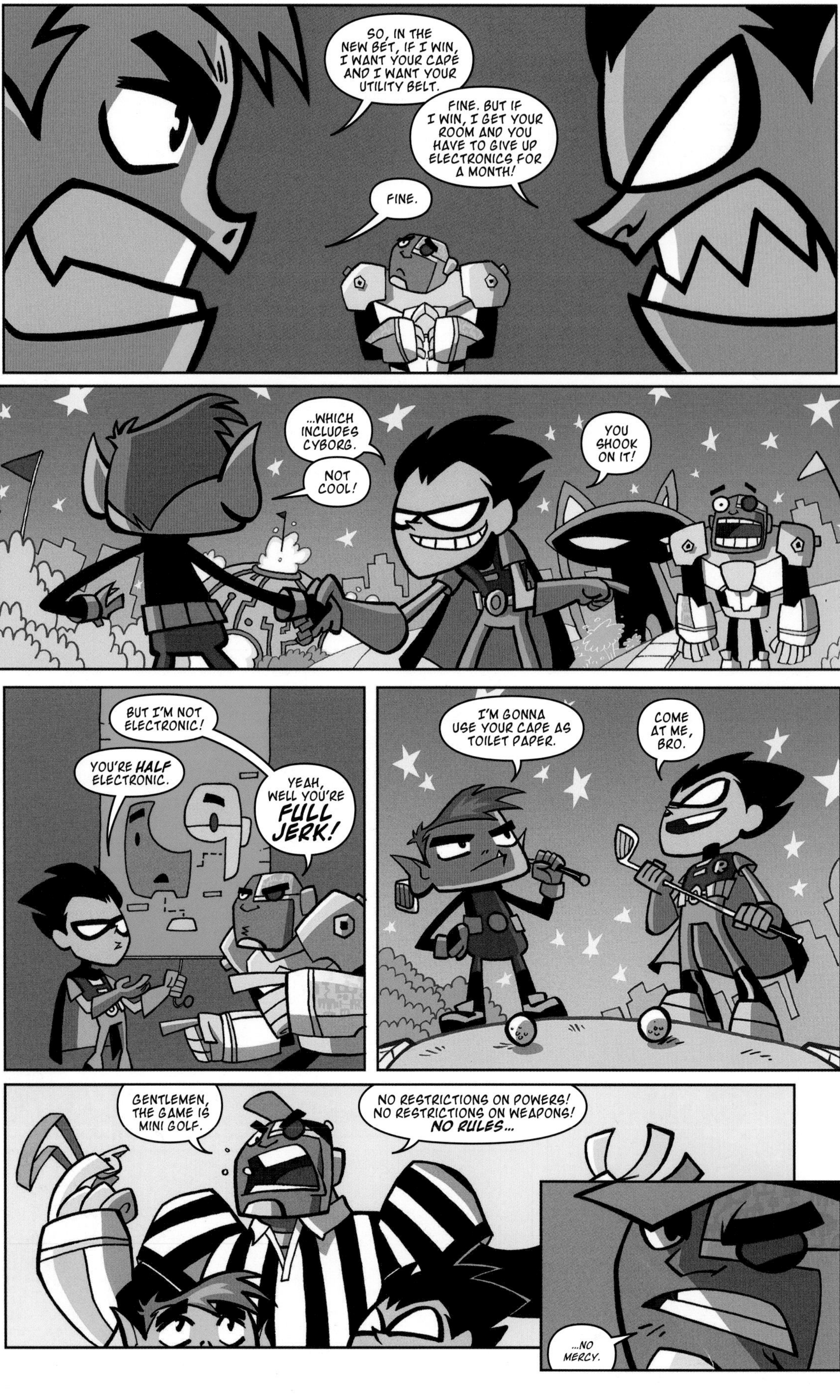
SO, IN THE NEW BET, IF I WIN, I WANT YOUR CAPE AND I WANT YOUR UTILITY BELT.
FINE. BUT IF I WIN, I GET YOUR ROOM AND YOU HAVE TO GIVE UP ELECTRONICS FOR A MONTH!
FINE.
...WHICH INCLUDES CYBORG.
NOT COOL!
YOU SHOOK ON IT!
BUT I'M NOT ELECTRONIC!
YOU'RE HALF ELECTRONIC.
YEAH, WELL YOU'RE FULL JERK!
I'M GONNA USE YOUR CAPE AS TOILET PAPER.
COME AT ME, BRO.
GENTLEMEN, THE GAME IS MINI GOLF.
NO RESTRICTIONS ON POWERS! NO RESTRICTIONS ON WEAPONS! NO RULES...
...NO MERCY.

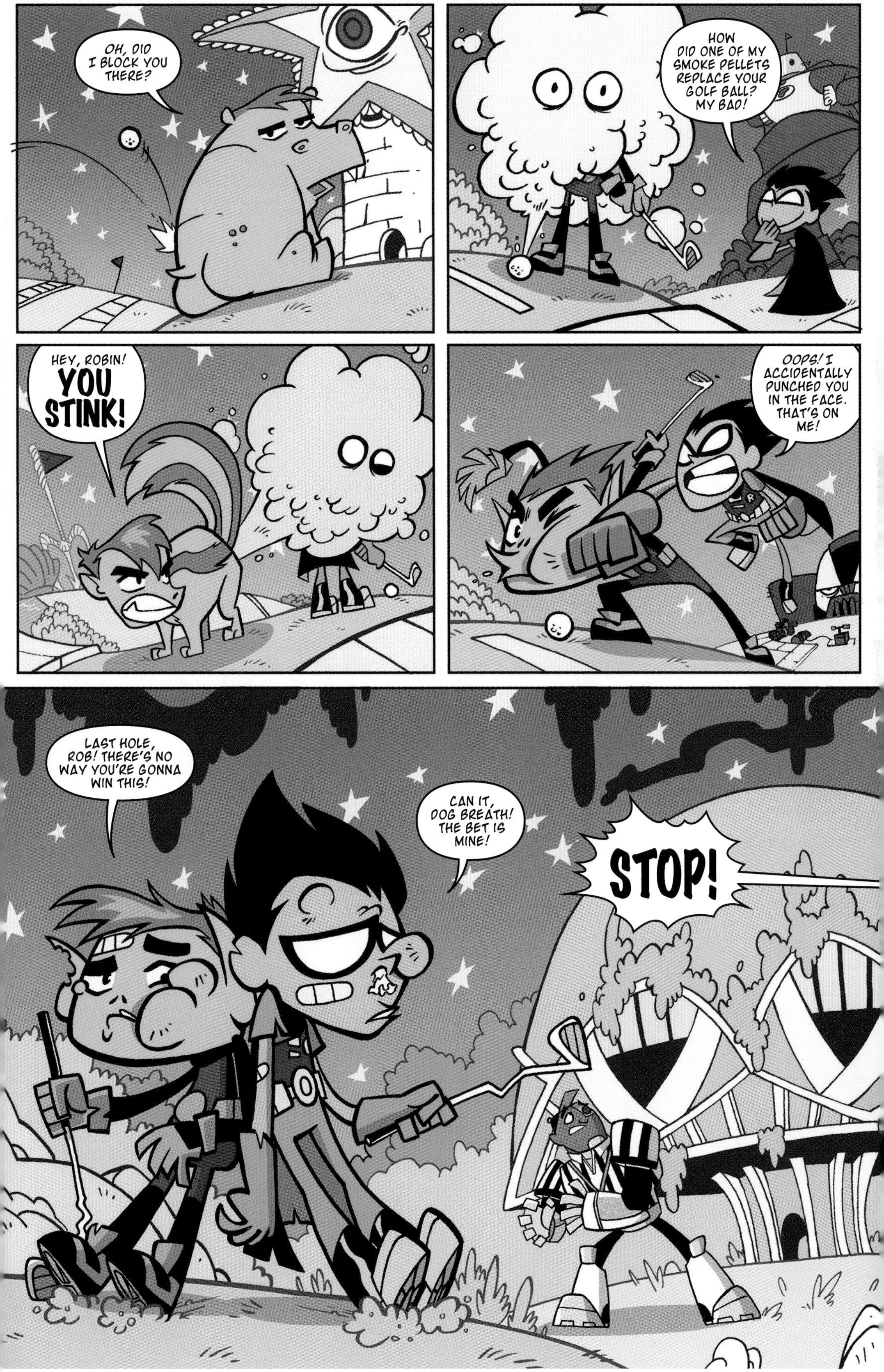
OH, DID I BLOCK YOU THERE?
HOW DID ONE OF MY SMOKE PELLETS REPLACE YOUR GOLF BALL? MY BAD!
HEY, ROBIN! YOU STINK!
OOPS! I ACCIDENTALLY PUNCHED YOU IN THE FACE. THAT'S ON ME!
LAST HOLE, ROB! THERE'S NO WAY YOU'RE GONNA WIN THIS!
CAN IT, DOG BREATH! THE BET IS MINE!
STOP!

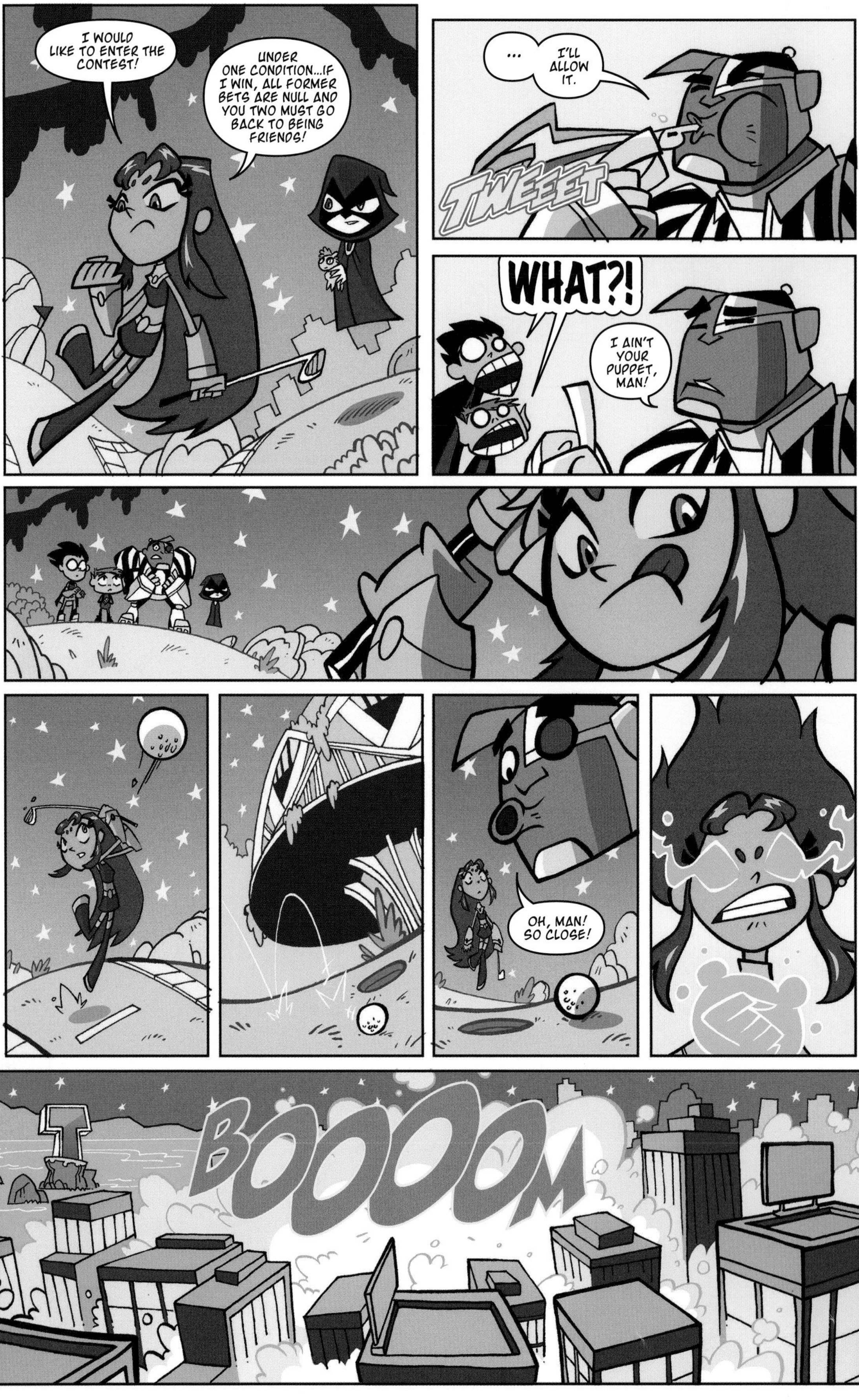
I WOULD LIKE TO ENTER THE CONTEST!
UNDER ONE CONDITION...IF I WIN, ALL FORMER BETS ARE NULL AND YOU TWO MUST GO BACK TO BEING FRIENDS!
...
I'LL ALLOW IT.
TWEEET
WHAT?!
I AIN'T YOUR PUPPET, MAN!
OH, MAN! SO CLOSE!
BOOOOM

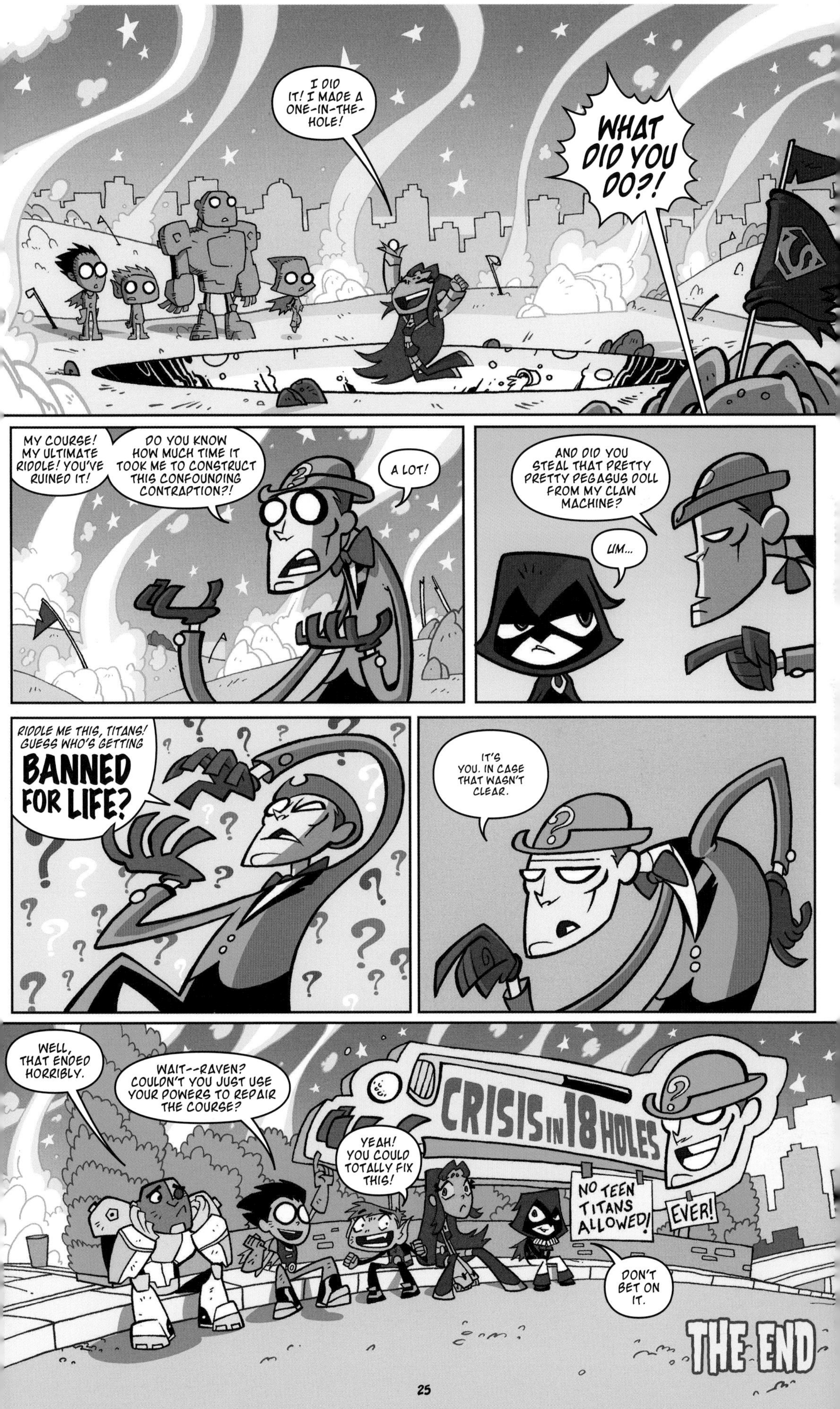
I DID IT! I MADE A ONE-IN-THE-HOLE!
WHAT DID YOU DO?!
MY COURSE! MY ULTIMATE RIDDLE! YOU'VE RUINED IT!
DO YOU KNOW HOW MUCH TIME IT TOOK ME TO CONSTRUCT THIS CONFOUNDING CONTRAPTION?!
A LOT!
AND DID YOU STEAL THAT PRETTY PRETTY PEGASUS DOLL FROM MY CLAW MACHINE?
UM...
RIDDLE ME THIS, TITANS! GUESS WHO'S GETTING BANNED FOR LIFE?
IT'S YOU. IN CASE THAT WASN'T CLEAR.
WELL, THAT ENDED HORRIBLY.
WAIT--RAVEN? COULDN'T YOU JUST USE YOUR POWERS TO REPAIR THE COURSE?
CRISIS IN 18 HOLES
YEAH! YOU COULD TOTALLY FIX THIS!
NO TEEN TITANS ALLOWED!
EVER!
DON'T BET ON IT.
THE END

CREATORS

SHOLLY FISCH

Bitten by a radioactive typewriter, Sholly Fisch has spent the wee hours writing books, comics, TV scripts, and online material for over 25 years. His comic book credits include more than 200 stories and features about characters such as Batman, Superman, Bugs Bunny, Daffy Duck, Spider-Man, and Ben 10. Currently, he writes stories for Action Comics every month, plus stories for Looney Tunes and Scooby-Doo. By day, Sholly is a mild-mannered developmental psychologist who helps to create educational TV shows, web sites, and other media for kids.

MERRILL HAGAN

Merrill Hagan is a writer who has worked on numerous episodes of the hit *Teen Titans Go!* TV show. In addition, he has authored several *Teen Titans Go!* comic books and was a writer for the original *Teen Titans* series in 2003.

BEN BATES

Ben Bates is a comic book illustrator, colorist, and writer. In addition to *Teen Titans Go!*, he has also worked on *Teenage Mutant Ninja Turtles*, *Mega Man*, *My Little Pony*, and many other comics.

JORGE CORONA

Jorge Corona is a Venezuelan comic artist who is well-known for his all-ages fantasy-adventure series *Feathers* and his work on *Jim Henson's The Storyteller: Dragons*. In addition to *Teen Titans Go!*, he has also worked on *Batman Beyond*, *Justice League Beyond*, *We Are Robin*, *Goners*, and many other comics.

GLOSSARY

accuse (uh-KYOOZ)—to say that someone has done something wrong

birthright (BURTH-rite)—a right or an object given to someone because the person is born into a specific family or group

compromise (KAHM-pruh-myz)—to agree to something that is not exactly what either side wants in order to make a decision

confound (kuhn-FOUND)—to cause surprise or confusion

conquer (KAHNG-kuhr)—to defeat and take control of an enemy

contraption (kuhn-TRAP-shuhn)—a strange or odd device or machine

demonic (dee-MON-ik)—having to do with evil spirits

dingus (DING-gus)—a word used humorously in place of the name of something

dojo (DOH-joh)—a martial arts training place

flimflam (FLIM-flam)—nonsensical talk

guardian (GAR-dee-uhn)—someone who carefully watches and protects something

hankering (HANG-kur-ing)—a hunger for something

infested (in-FESS-tid)—filled with pests

kimono (kee-MOH-noh)—a long, loose robe with wide sleeves and a sash

mutant (MYOOT-uhnt)—a living thing that has developed different characteristics than its parents had

objective (uhb-JEK-tiv)—an aim or goal that you are working toward

penetrate (PEN-uh-trate)—to go inside or through something

possession (puh-ZESH-uhn)—to own or control something

renounce (ri-NOWNS)—to formally reject a belief

restriction (ri-STRIK-shun)—a rule or limitation

technique (tek-NEEK)—a method or a way of doing something that requires skill

vanquish (VANG-kwish)—to defeat or conquer an enemy in battle

witness (WIT-niss)—a person who has seen or heard something

VISUAL QUESTIONS & WRITING PROMPTS

1. Based on their facial expressions, what emotions or feelings are each Teen Titan experiencing in this panel?

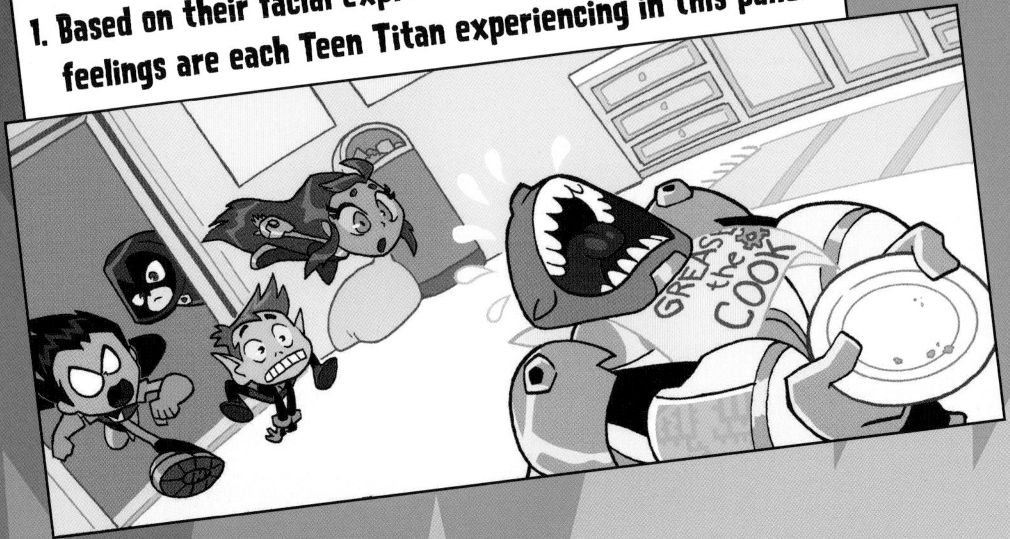
GREASY the COOK

2. At the end of the first story, Silkie changes after eating the pizza. Write a short story describing what happens next!

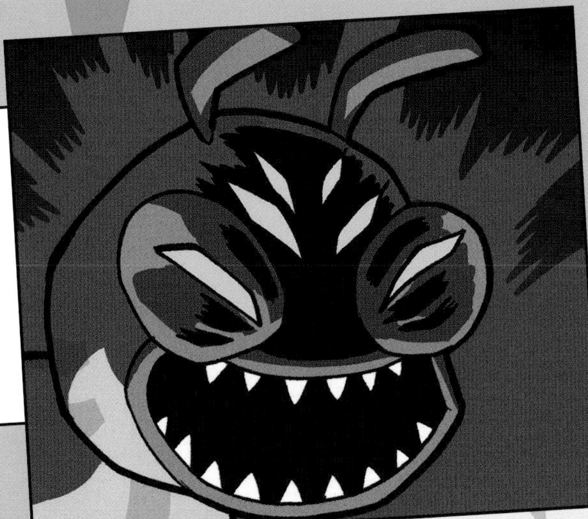

3. Why does Beast Boy turn into an elephant to play mini-golf? How do Cyborg and Robin feel about his transformation?

4. Why is Cyborg wearing this costume? What does it tell you about his role in the story?

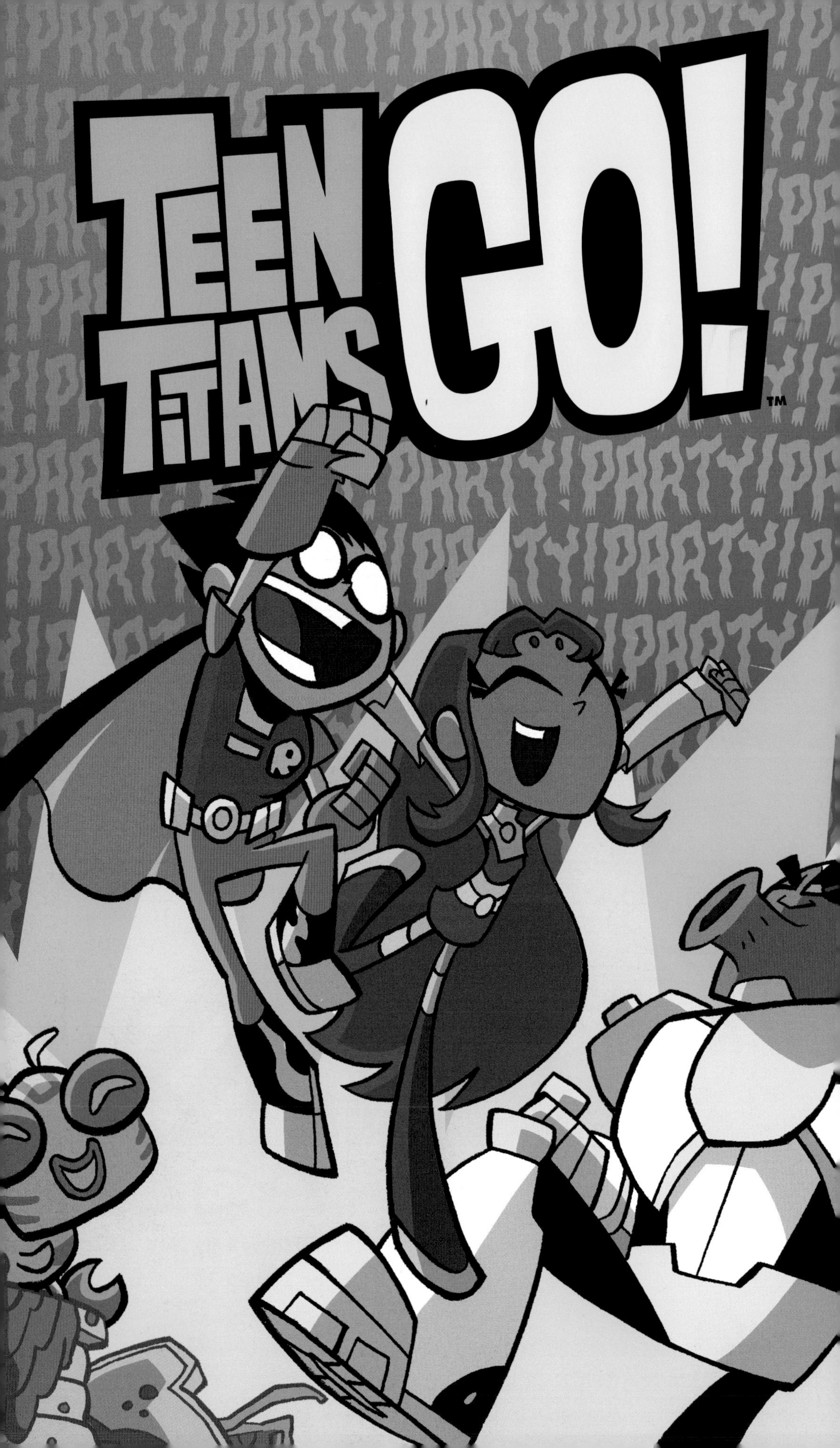
TEEN TITANS GO!™
PARTY! PARTY! PARTY!

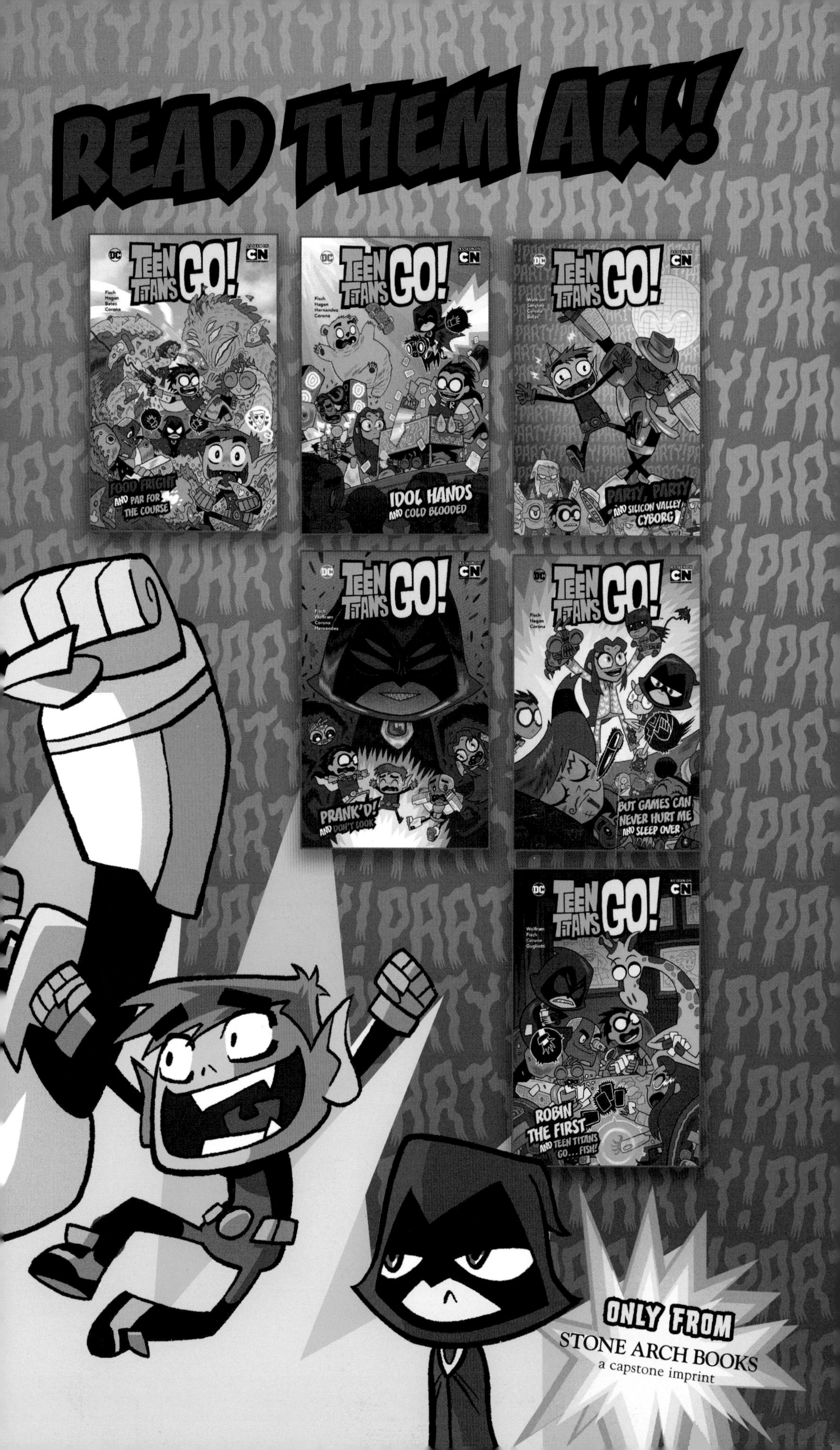

READ THEM ALL!
TEEN TITANS GO!
FOOD FRIGHT AND PAR FOR THE COURSE
IDOL HANDS AND COLD BLOODED
PARTY, PARTY AND SILICON VALLEY CYBORG
PRANK'D! AND DON'T LOOK
BUT GAMES CAN NEVER HURT ME AND SLEEP OVER
ROBIN THE FIRST AND TEEN TITANS GO... FISH!
ONLY FROM
STONE ARCH BOOKS
a capstone imprint

TEEN TITANS GO!™

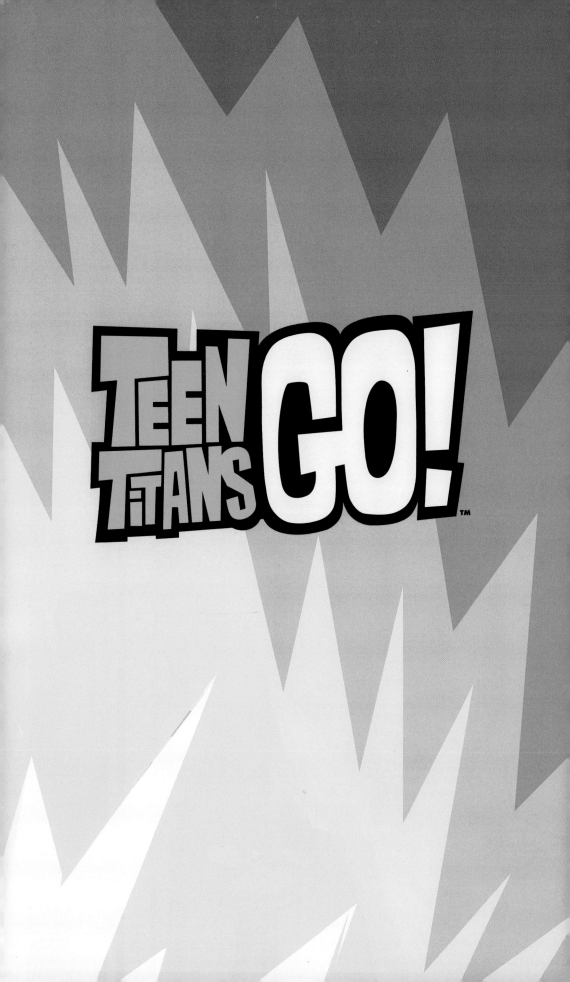